Suffolk's Last Cold War

Suffolk's Last Cc
Victim

WARNING

THIS STORY IS NOT ABOUT THE PHYSICAL ASPECT OF THE COLD WAR.

IT IS ABOUT THE UNEXPECTED CONSEQUENCES OF THIS WAR

Author

Tony Harris

Suffolk
Born and bred

Suffolk's Last Cold War Victim

Foreword

By

Charlie Haylock

"This is an intriguing thriller written in a typical Suffolk storytelling way . . . . a main theme with little asides along the way which help to build a picture, create plots and subplots as the story unfolds and then climaxes with an unsuspecting end.

George Mitchell's world has ended . . . and then . . . due to a dramatic unforeseen occurrence, his life changes in such a way . . . it would never be the same again."

Suffolk's Last Cold War Victim

Acknowledgements

I would like to thank the following people who have helped me in the writing of this novel.

Charlie Haylock. *For Suffolkating the script and giving me help and support.*
Ruth Gitsham. *My Proof reader*
Tracy. *My darling wife, whose support and encouragement helped me through this project.*
Jamie. *My son he helped to format and design the book cover.*
Vicki. *My daughter, she was the first person to read the book and provide some good feedback.*
Lesley Dolphin. *Lesley kindly allowed me to talk about my book on her BBC Radio Suffolk afternoon programme with Charlie Haylock.*

'Thank yer koindly tergither'

This is a work of fiction. Names, characters, places and incidents are either the product of the authors' imaginations or are used fictitiously, and any resemblance to actual persons, living or dead, or to actual events or locales is entirely coincidental.

Suffolk's Last Cold War Victim

Chapter	Page
1. How did it come to this	5
2. Major opportunity	9
3. Disgruntled Pensioners	24
4. Extra, extra read all about it.	42
5. The trial	48
6. What's going on?	57
7. New beginnings	69
8. The new kid in town	80
9. The local darts match	88
10. The little bugger's brigade	92
11. Kindred spirits	100
12. That place north of Diss	104
13. More villagers' secrets	116
14. New friends and hidden talents	126
15. Births Deaths and Marriages	131
16. The Orford merman	144
17. Honesty is the best policy	155
18. Where's Jamie Oliver when you want him?	165
19. Some furreners want to meet you	171
20. Only a few people have the gift	180
21. A village in shock	193
22. Peace at last	210
23. Password to paradise	220

Suffolk's Last Cold War Victim

Chapter 1

How Did It Come To This?

April 1st 2018, is a dull, bitterly cold morning. George Mitchell is on his knees, begging forgiveness from his wife Susan and their son Jason, for what he is about to say and do. This is not an April Fools wind-up but, oh how he wishes it was.

He begins explaining why he is leaving them to start a new life in a different part of the country. He tells them he has made arrangements with Susan's brother Simon to take care of their needs.

The pain of this task is making him feel physically sick; he knows they deserve an explanation as to why he is leaving them. Between the sobs he manages to mutter, 'Please believe me when I tell you, I'll love you both for the rest of my life'. Unable to speak any more, he just stares at them, hoping by the look on his face they will understand his reasons for going away.

After a few minutes, he senses they have accepted the situation and given him their consent. Wiping away his tears, he rises and takes a couple of steps back to have a final look at the epitaph on their headstone.

Suffolk's Last Cold War Victim

Here lie the bodies of my beloved Wife
Susan Mitchell
Aged 47
21/05/1971-14/2/2018
And Son
Jason Mitchell
12/01/1997-14/2/2018
Aged 21
Both taken tragically from this world
Now safe in the arms of God
And forever in my thoughts

The headstone was commissioned and paid for by a good friend of George's. It normally takes between to 5-6 months, but due to these exceptional circumstances it was given special preference

The rest of their family and close friends, having said their goodbyes exit the cemetery, leaving George alone with his thoughts. He turns and looks to the headstone immediately opposite and said, 'Mum, Dad please take care of them. I love and miss you both.' He begins walking away, but cannot help looking back every few steps to his loved ones, not knowing when he will be able to visit them again.

The funeral was given special permission to be held on a Sunday, to confuse the gang waiting to get even with him. Waiting for him at the gates of Manor Park cemetery are several armed police and his good friend, Craig Ferguson. Craig wraps his arms around his friend's shoulders, hugging

Suffolk's Last Cold War Victim

him tightly. George is still sobbing uncontrollably as Craig said, 'Come on old mate, I'll treat you to a stiff drink or two'.

Craig Ferguson is a Metropolitan Detective Chief Inspector. He joined the police force in September 1990. Because of his height, he is 5'-7", George calls him 'Laptop' as he is a small PC.

On the evidence of George and Craig's investigation, the Crown Prosecution Service successfully prosecuted a criminal gang led by a fraudulent financier and his Bulgarian mistress.

In the nearby Red Lion public house, they enjoy a few pints of George's favourite tipple, 'Ghost Ship' bitter. George sighs and says, 'Craig, I wish I'd never heard that bastard Trevor Bannister's name and never taken on that job. But I did and now I've got to live with the consequences.' This is first time he has heard George using a swear word. Craig tries to change his mood by asking him about his planned move to Suffolk.

After a third pint of beer, George tells Craig 'Me and Susan became sweethearts soon after we met in the first year of high school. We were both very shy, especially in the company of others, but our support for each other got us through our school and teenage years.

We're both committed Christians and attended the same local church services together. My sense of good versus evil, right and wrong, led me to a career fighting injustice. In 1989, at the age of eighteen, I applied to join the Police force. I was unsuccessful because of my height; at 5'-7" I was below

Suffolk's Last Cold War Victim

the 5'-10" minimum height requirement unlike you, who was accepted a year later when the height restrictions were abolished.

With Susan's encouragement, I got a job in journalism with a local newspaper. I worked hard over the next four years, gaining experience in all aspects of the publishing business. One day my editor asked me to investigate a gang rumoured to be selling illicit cigarettes in the local area.

My editor was very pleased with my efforts, especially when the scoop made the national press. I was pleased the gang's activities had been duly punished with some receiving jail terms. I knew this was the type of journalism I wanted to concentrate on.

I continued working for the newspaper for the next two years, but further investigative jobs were in short supply. At twenty-four years of age, with the full agreement of Susan, I resigned and began working freelance.

My work for other newspapers grew slowly at first, but soon my reputation for attention to detail and reliability meant I was never short of offers of work.

Within my first year of freelance working, I was earning enough money to ensure a comfortable lifestyle and financial security. This was just as well as Susan announced she was pregnant with our first child and would be finishing work in a few months. I was really excited with this news; the love for my wife had never been greater than at that moment.'

Suffolk's Last Cold War Victim

Chapter 2

Major opportunity

9 months earlier

On Friday 21st July 2017, George receives a telephone call from Mark Haines the editor of a well- known Sunday newspaper, The World of News. He asks if he would be interested in interviewing some victims of a Pensions fraud. As George did not have anything ongoing at that moment, he agrees to meet him at 10:00 am on Monday 24th July.

At the meeting, Mark informs George, 'An officer friend of mine in the Metropolitan Police has asked me for a favour. The Met Fraud Squad has received reports from a number of elderly pensioners saying they've fallen victim to a pension fraud.

The officer said he'd been heading up the investigation before it was put on hold due to a large number of other serious fraud cases. As a consequence, he was reassigned to a higher profile case by senior management. He's very unhappy, having spent many hours investigating this crime and seeing first-hand the suffering those poor people have been going through.

He said if we, the paper, continue interviewing the victims for him, he'll let us know when and where arrests are to be made. We'll be in pole position to go to print, as the

Suffolk's Last Cold War Victim

stories will already have been written. Your job will be interviewing the victims, gathering background information leading up to the fraud and the effect it's having on their lives.

I don't have a lot to give you, other than the victim's details and the name of the company involved, Simon Stone Associates. The address on the company's paperwork doesn't exist and the phone number is now unobtainable.

A number of victims have given us permission for you to interview them, so if you want this case, it's yours. Oh, one small thing. One of the victims told my friend that Simon Stone received a phone call during their meeting. He went into the hallway to answer it. The pensioner overheard him talking about a Globe or Robe Tower on the Isle of Dogs. It's probably something of nothing. And this is the amount I'm prepared to pay you.'

George looks at the figures on a piece of paper Mark has just handed him. Without hesitation, George said, 'I'll take it and make a start right away. I know the area well and there's definitely a Globe Tower there.' Flicking through the details, he makes a quick calculation and said, 'I believe I can arrange to get all the interviews and statements done, printed and on your desk in four weeks, if that's OK with you?' Mark replies, 'Absolutely fine by me. All I ask is that you provide me with a weekly update.' With that they shook hands to close the deal and George goes home to begin making plans.

Something keeps niggling him and breaking his train of thought. It's the little snippet of information regarding Globe Tower. He decides to check it out first thing in the morning

Suffolk's Last Cold War Victim

before going to his office to arrange the interviews. George rents an office at 154A Old Broad St. near Liverpool St. Station.

The next morning George arrives outside the Globe Tower office block. He goes inside and speaks to the receptionist. She confirms Simon Stone Associates have never been registered in this office block.

As his leaves the building, he takes a photograph of a board listing all the companies trading in the tower. His eye is drawn to the 6th floor where he sees the name, Trevor Bannister Pension Broker, the only company involved in pensions. Could this be a lead or just a coincidence?

Before going to his office he goes into a small café opposite and orders a cup of coffee. Drinking his coffee he looks down the list of people he needs to contact, he stops at Colonel Geoffrey Hungerford from Suffolk. He decides to call him first to arrange a meeting.

George introduces himself saying he is acting on behalf of The World of News newspaper, regarding a pension fraud by Simon Stone Associates.

During the conversation they agree a date and time to meet. George asks, 'Colonel Hungerford, would it be possible for you to give me a description of the man who claimed to be Simon Stone when he visited you in 2013? I know it's a long time ago.'

The Colonel replies 'I hope you've got a pen and a long piece of paper. Tell me when you're ready.' With that, he begins to reel off an almost forensic description of the man.

Suffolk's Last Cold War Victim

'Height 5-11", weight 13 ½ stone, age early to mid 40s, greying short hair, light blue eyes, tanned complexion, natural not a fake spray on, pointed jaw, he has a small wart-like growth on the left-hand side of his nose.

He was wearing a dark blue pin stripe suit. He has a deep, rasping cockney accent which he tries to disguise. He also has a slight limp on his left leg. I hope this helps you find the bastard who ruined my life.'

George replies, 'I'm truly thankful for this information and I look forward to seeing you in person next week.'

Looking out of the window onto the street he nearly chokes on his coffee, as a man fitting the description he's just been given including the limp, walks past the café. He watches as he crosses the road and enters the Globe Tower building. Perhaps it had not been a coincidence after all.

Composing himself, he quickly crosses the road and re-enters the building. He arrives just in time to see the man enter a lift, he is the only occupant. He stands back as the doors close and watches the lift going up. It eventually stops at the 6th floor before descending again. He hopes this is the breakthrough he needs, but what should he do next?

He knows the man fits the description given to him by the Colonel. This however was from 4 years ago. What about his voice? He decides to use the public phone in reception to call Trevor Bannister's office number. The phone rings twice before a man with a deep cockney accent answers, 'Trevor Bannister speaking, can I help you?' George replies, 'I'm so sorry, I've dialled a wrong number, sorry to bother you.' before replacing the handset.

'That's it. I think I've found Simon Stone. I can't believe it. That's so lucky,' he mutters to himself. He looks at his watch it is 10:35 am. His mind is going ten to the dozen because he knows there are so many questions he has to answer before he can move on.

- Simon Stone and Trevor Bannister are they one and the same?
- Who else, if anyone, is involved in these fraudulent activities?
- Apart from the people in his dossier, how many other victims are there?
- How much money is involved and where has it gone?
- With this information, will 4 weeks be long enough to complete the task?

George phones his wife to tell her he may be late home this evening, as he wants to shadow Bannister today. Susan is not a bit surprised; she is used to receiving this type of call.

He looks around for somewhere to sit and work, but still see Bannister when he leaves the building. Just behind the reception desk, there is a communal seating area for workers to use during their lunch break. This is ideal as he can work at a table with a good view of the front doors.

He uses the time to phone round some of his acquaintances in the financial markets. He needs to find as much information as he can on Simon Stone/ Trevor Bannister. No-one has heard of Simon Stone, but a few recognise the name, Trevor Bannister.

Suffolk's Last Cold War Victim

They describe him as an ordinary run of the mill, hardworking pension broker. He clients are all within a ten mile radius of his office and he is not known to be reckless with his dealings in the marketplace. Suddenly, he has big doubts whether this man is indeed the callous, calculating, cheating piece of scum who has been ruining these pensioner's lives for years. Then he remembers the Colonel's description, which reminds him of other cases he has worked on, where butter wouldn't melt in some of those villain's mouths.

At 15:30 pm he spots Bannister walking past the reception desk heading for the exit doors. George follows him maintaining a safe distance between them.

He follows him to South Quay train station, where he boards a Docklands Light Railway train to Bank Station, before changing to a Central train to Liverpool Street Station.

George manages to take several pictures en route without raising any suspicions. He boards a Greater Anglia train, alighting a few stops later at Manor Park. George is pleasantly surprised as this is his local station.

He follows him on foot for a few hundred yards before Bannister turns into the drive of a large detached house in Aldersbrook Road. In the driveway there are two cars: a 2015 registered black BMW X3, the second a 2013 registered grey Hyundai I30. Incredibly this is less than a mile and a half from George's own home in Carlyle Road.

Arriving home he unlocks his front door and shouts, 'I hope you're decent my little Trojan horse.' This is his pet name for Susan, as she would unleash a hidden army on anyone who threatened her family. Susan is surprised to see

Suffolk's Last Cold War Victim

her husband so early and replies, 'Hello darling lovely to see you so soon. I haven't got anything prepared yet, so you'll have to take me out to dinner.' As it has been a productive day, he is more than pleased to earn some brownie points by treating his wife to dinner.

Early the next morning George drives to Bannister's home and parks up 50 yards away. He isn't sure if Bannister is walking to the station, getting a lift or using his own car. At 08:15 am he sees Bannister exit his house through the front door and begin walking in the direction of the station. George waits a few minutes before driving to the stations car park.

Waiting on platform 4, he is relieved to see his target walk onto the same platform. They both board the train to Liverpool Street.

When the train arrives at Liverpool St. station, they both disembark. George watches as Bannister enters Starbucks and orders a cup of coffee. When he receives his drink he sits at a table next to a young woman. She appears to know him by the way they are talking and looking at each other. George's journalistic instincts kick in as he mutters, 'Something's not right here.' 15 minutes later Bannister having finished his drink leaves for his office.

George needs to find out more about Bannister's business and lifestyle. He decides to return to his office, where he will have more privacy. He trawls through the internet, Facebook and other social media sites but cannot find anything untoward.

Bannister appears to be in a stable marital relationship with his wife, Samantha and their two teenage daughters. His mind goes back to this morning's meeting with the young

Suffolk's Last Cold War Victim

woman in Starbucks. If George's suspicions are right, this has 'extramarital affair' written all over it. He knows Mark Haines will welcome any salacious scandal as 'icing on the cake' and maybe give him a bonus on completion.

The rest of the day is spent arranging meetings with pensioners in the Simon Stone Associates dossier. He makes a list of those prepared to be interviewed at his office and those requiring a home visit. Only one person Mr Dean Barns agrees to meet him in his office on Monday of the third week.

The second week will be filled with interviews around the country. He arranges them in an anticlockwise direction, starting in the north before ending up in East Anglia.

George has niggling doubts regarding the young woman in Starbucks. She's waiting for Bannister once again on Thursday. He gambles on them meeting again tomorrow.

Arriving thirty minutes earlier than the previous days, his gamble pays off when he spots the woman walking into the café. He walks behind her as she makes her way to the counter. The woman is very pretty, quite tall, slim with long black hair. He guesses she is in her late twenties to early thirties. George listens as she orders her drink, she spoke with an eastern European accent.

Bannister arrives and sits down next to her. As they chat together, the woman gives Bannister a folder. He opens it and takes out a number of papers. He holds each one up in front of him to read them. George counts fifteen pages, Bannister signs five of them. As George is sitting directly behind him he is able to film, photograph and record their conversations using a modified mobile phone. Similar to ones

Suffolk's Last Cold War Victim

used by undercover investigators during surveillance operations.

He replaced the papers into the folder and handed it back to the young woman. Bannister gives her a peck on the cheek before leaving, presumably heading to his office.

George quickly decides to concentrate on the woman today. He wants to find anything that will help him identify her, where she works, her name and where she lives?

Leaving Starbucks the woman makes her way to platform 6 and boards the 10:07 am Greater Anglia train to Cambridge North. He has no idea where she is taking him, but he is quite excited to think she may be the chink in Bannister's armour and proves to be the breakthrough he is looking for.

During the journey she is constantly talking and texting on her mobile phone. He is close enough to hear, but as she is talking in a foreign language, he cannot understand what she is saying. Once again, he uses his device to record her conversations.

One hour and twenty minutes later, they both step off the train at Cambridge North Station. He follows her out of the station to a car park, where she unlocks a red Range Rover Discovery. He makes a note of the registration number AY17 DQX and the name of the dealer who sold it, Bernard's of Downham Market. He now has some photos and a car registration number to help him identify her.

He returns to his office and using one of his vast arrays of 'Insider Friends' he phones Marcus Norris. He works for the DVLA, 'Hi Marcus, this is George Mitchell.' Marcus answers, 'Hello George, how can I help you?' George said, 'I'm hoping

Suffolk's Last Cold War Victim

you can give me some information on a vehicle, I believe is being used in a fraud case I'm working on. I can get the police to authorise this check if you like.'

Marcus knows and trusts George and says, 'No problems, what's the registration number? 'It's a red Range Rover, AV17 DQX. The dealer is BERNARDS of Downham Market. Marcus types the details in the data system, a few minutes later he replies, 'Right it's actually on hire to a company, Fenland Farms, the name on the rental document is IVANKA DUMITRU, who's registered at Fen Farm, New Road, Downham Market, PE34 9AB.

Ashley writes down the name and address before saying, 'That's very interesting, thanks for your help mate, speak to you soon.' As tomorrow is a Saturday he once again gambles she wouldn't be travelling to London. The gamble pays off, when he spots the Range Rover parked in the driveway of a farmhouse at the address in Downham Market.

Fen Farm appears to be mainly agricultural, by the number of farm vehicles and storage barns around the farmhouse.

He parks in a lay-by about 100 yards away. From here he can see all movements in and out of the farm and as the terrain is very flat, he has good views of the surrounding area.

Pretending to be a bird spotter, he uses his camera, fitted with a telescopic lens, to take photos of all the buildings and fields on both sides of the road. He pays special attention to the large number of caravans and their occupants; this however is to be expected in a farming environment.

Suffolk's Last Cold War Victim

Just after 12:15 pm he sees the Range Rover drive out of the driveway, heading towards him. Ivanka is driving, just as he hoped. Keeping a good distance between them, he follows her for the next five miles before she turns into a narrow lane. Viewing his Satnav, he sees it is a dead-end road that leads to a farm a quarter of a mile away. He spots a petrol station about two hundred yards away and decides to park up and wait until she reappears.

Thirty minutes later he spots her car as it exits the farm. He follows her as she turns back towards Downham Market. Arriving in the town centre, she parks in the road outside Beechams, a hairdressing/ beautician salon. Only then does George spot a young woman with long black hair, carrying a small suitcase get out of the rear passenger door.

They both enter the salon and go straight into a room towards the back. Ten minutes later, Ivanka returns to her car alone and drives off. The girl obviously isn't a customer, so what is she doing in there?

Back in her car, she heads out of town along the A1101 for another six miles, before turning left at a signpost indicating Pond Hall Farm. He believes this is another agricultural farm, as the nearby fields are filled with arable crops.

At 14:10 she drives out of the farm, continuing along the A1101, until reaching the main street in Wisbech. She turns into a small Pay and Display car park. He drives in and parks a few places behind before following her on foot. She walks to another hairdressing salon. Again, she goes into a backroom, reappearing twenty minutes later. Whilst waiting for her to return, he quickly returns to his car and changes his T shirt and blue V neck jumper to a white shirt, tie and jacket.

Suffolk's Last Cold War Victim

Resuming his pursuit, George is pleased when the woman enters the nearby Barley Mow pub and orders something to eat and drink. He sits immediately behind the woman as she eats her meal. He can hear her speaking on her phone, mostly in a foreign language and once again he records and films her conversations.

During one phone call she speaks in English. He hears her arranging to meet a man at Fen Farm this evening. His heart almost skips a beat, when he hears her say to the man, 'Trevor darling, what time are you arriving? I can't wait for us to spend the whole night together.'

As the woman prepares to leave the pub, George quickly makes his way back to the car park, in readiness to follow her to her next destination. He did not have long to wait before she appears and begins driving along the A47 heading north, before exiting onto Wiggenhall Road.

Two miles along this road she turns right into a long drive. As there are no signposts to show where it will take her, George decides to pull over parking on a large grass verge. From the map on his Satnav, he sees the road leads to Brick House Farm.

He gets out of the car with his camera and a can of drink. Standing behind a hedge, he begins taking pictures of the farmhouse across the field.

Just then, he spots a young man working a few yards away in the field. George calls out, 'Hello. Would you like a can of drink?' The man jumps back in surprise and walks towards him. Once again, George asked him if would like a drink. Only when George waves the can towards him, the man

Suffolk's Last Cold War Victim

understands what is on offer and begins to smile and takes the can from him.

George tries to start a conversation with the man, using a combination of talking and hand gestures. 'Do you work here?' the man nods to indicate he does. For the next ten minutes he tries to communicate with the man, but concedes this is a lost cause.

The man becomes very agitated when he spots the Range Rover driving back down the drive; he shouts out in a similar accent to the woman 'No talkie, no talkie.' Quickly turning away, he returns to his duties.

George jumps back into his car as the woman drives by. There are no further stops as she drives back to Fen Farm, arriving late in the afternoon. George once again parks up in a place that gives him a good view of the farmhouse. Everything he has witnessed today raises more questions than he has answers for. The only thing that can definitely be answered today is the identity of 'Trevor,' the man Ivanka is meeting this evening.

He does not have long to wait, as just after 18:00 pm. a black BMW X3 drives up to the farmhouse. George begins taking photographs of the man as he gets out of his car and is greeted with a long kiss and cuddle by Ivanka, before they both go into the farmhouse.

George returns to his car and reviews the photographs he has just taken; they captured a lot of sexual emotion between them. Feeling physically and mentally drained, he

Suffolk's Last Cold War Victim

decides to call it a day and drives back home to review his first week's findings.

He makes a list of questions he desperately needs answering.

Trevor Bannister

- What is the connection, if any, between him and Simon Stone Associates?
- What is his relationship with Ivanka Dumitru?
- What is the significance of the papers he signed in the coffee shop?

Ivanka Dumitru

- Is this her real name or an alias?
- Why was she visiting the farms and hairdressing salons?
- Who was the young girl she took to the salon?
- What is her relationship with Trevor Bannister?
- Why was the man in the field so spooked when he spotted her car?
- What will the telephone conversations I recorded in the pub reveal when they have been translated?

Arriving home in the evening, George rings Mark Haines to give him an update. As usual he keeps his report as short and concise as possible, mainly because of the number of questions he still has to find answers to.

He tells Mark, 'I've got concerns I may've stumbled on a number of other crimes, not just the fraud case. If this is true, I'm worried my findings may compromise any police

Suffolk's Last Cold War Victim

investigations'. Mark reassures him 'Don't worry the paper won't do anything that could jeopardise the case'. George is relieved with his reply.

George emails Mark the photographs of Bannister and Dumitru kissing passionately outside the farmhouse and said he believes they may be having an extramarital affair. Mark let out a little yelp and said, 'Great, you know what this means don't you?' George knows exactly what it means, and he looks forward to spending it.

Mark asks George to forward the film and voice recordings to him, so he can have them translated ready for their next meeting on Friday. Mark finishes with, 'Great work, George. I'll think about what you've said and if needs be, I'll invite someone from the Met to attend our meeting. Once again, George feels reassured.

Suffolk's Last Cold War Victim

Chapter 3

Disgruntled Pensioners

George's plans this week are to travel the country, interviewing Simon Stone Associates' victims. He decides to work anticlockwise, starting from the north on Monday, the west Tuesday, and the south on Wednesday, ending up in the east on Thursday.

The family attends the Sunday morning church service, before returning home for an early roast dinner. After saying goodbye to his family George sets off on the long journey to Gateshead. He will spend the night in a local Travelodge, before his first appointment on Monday morning.

The first person on his agenda is Philip Parker, a retired prison governor from Gateshead. He meets him at his local working men's club. They go into a small dressing room behind the stage, where they will have some privacy.

Philip asks George if he wants a drink. He asks for a cup of tea, he has another two meetings today and would never contemplate drinking and driving.

Philip explains, prior to his retirement he requested an estimate from his pension provider. He was slightly disappointed as their forecast figures, were less than the ideal amount he had in mind. He discussed this with Nick Stirton, a former colleague, who had retired himself two years previously. Nick told Philip he had invested his lump sum with

Suffolk's Last Cold War Victim

a Pensions Broker named Simon Stone. He received good dividends on his first year's investment. With this recommendation, Philip contacted Simon Stone in 2014, who agreed to meet him at his home to discuss his options.

He tells George 'Stone made a good impression on me, as he hadn't been pushy. He answered all my questions satisfactorily and I was happy with the projected forecast of returns on my investment. As I didn't feel pressured, I agreed to invest the whole of my £120k lump sum, with forecast returns between £7,500 (6 %) and £9,000 (7.5%) per annum. These figures were comparable to the figures my friend had been quoted.

Over the next three years, the dividends were slightly below forecast, but because of the state of the world's economy around this time, it was to be expected. Then due to unforeseen circumstances in February 2017 I needed to terminate my policy, and withdraw the money I'd invested. My wife of forty-two years announced she was leaving me and wanted a divorce, so I needed the money to pay her off as part of the divorce settlement. I'd hoped to pay her off and keep the house

I never had a reply to any of the correspondence I sent them, and the telephone number was always unobtainable. As a consequence, we've got to sell our home and split whatever we get between us.'

George thanks Philip for seeing him and gives him an assurance he will do everything possible to expose the culprits and get some, if not all his money back.

Suffolk's Last Cold War Victim

His next appointment is in Durham with Mr. Andrew Denny, a former Headmaster at a local primary school. George arrives on time and is shown into the front room of a three-bed detached house in a modern estate on the eastern area of the city.

George listens to the story of a man who invested a large part of his pension lump sum (£65k), with Simon Stone Associates in 2014. He made it clear to Simon Stone that this would be a 3-year investment plan, whilst waiting for other investments to mature. He and his wife intend to use the money to immigrate to Australia to be closer to their daughter and grandchildren. Now their dream move will not be possible and the stress of it all has severely affected his wife's health.

As with Philip Parker in March 2017, when the 3-year period was completed, Andrew tried everything possible to contact Simon Stone Associates, but was unable to do so. He reported the situation to the police, but felt they had let him down. He said trying to get any information from them was harder than contacting Simon Stone.

He became aware via social media a number of other pensioners were also having similar problems. He made contact with several of them, and they agreed he should become their spokesperson.

Again, George thanks his host for meeting him today, and assures him he will do everything in his power to bring this matter to a head as soon as possible.

Just as he is about to leave, George shows Andrew a photo of Trevor Bannister. 'Do you recognise the man in the

Suffolk's Last Cold War Victim

photograph, if so was he travelling alone?' Andrew replies immediately, 'That's Simon Stone and there was a woman with him. She dropped him off and collected him when we'd concluded the deal.'

Opening his laptop again, he selects photographs of his wife, his neighbour and Ivanka. He asks Andrew if he can identify any of these women as the driver of the car. Without hesitation he points to Ivanka.

George leaves Andrew with some good news, 'Due to your help I think I've positively identified Simon Stone.' The news immediately lifts the poor man's spirits. George is equally enthused, as he makes his way to Sedgefield for his final appointment of the day.

After stopping at a service station on the A1 (M) for a light lunch, he continues to his next appointment with Miss Isobel Grayson, a retired Headmistress. She insists he calls her Bella. Bella lives with her sister Shannon, a retired maternity nurse, in a three bed cottage close to Sedgefield racecourse.

The elderly couple brings George a cup of tea and some homemade fruit scones. A thankful George said, 'These are the best scones I've ever tasted.'

He begins taking notes of Bella's meeting with Simon Stone in April 2015. It is the same story he has already heard twice today. Although the amount invested is a lot less than the first two, to Bella £36k is still a large amount of money to lose, especially at her time of life.

Suffolk's Last Cold War Victim

Their only source of income now is their state pensions and a carers' allowance paid to Shannon, for looking after Bella, who has a serious heart condition.

With the interview over George is finishing another drink and scone. He wants to understand the human consequences the fraud has taken on the ladies. George's instinct for a story pays off when he begins asking some probing questions. It was Bella who admits, 'Shannon and I aren't really sisters we're lovers.'

Shannon said, 'George things are so very different today. Being gay now doesn't carry the stigma it once did. We were lovers in a time when being gay was considered a sin. In desperation I changed my surname by deed poll from Clements to Grayson, so we could live together and people would assume we are sisters. Now I use the name with pride, as we're married to each other.' George said 'I'm really happy for you both. You did what was right for you, not for those who can't appreciate true love.'

They continue telling him about their lives together. Towards the end of the meeting George asks Bella to look at a photo of Bannister. She confirms, 'That's the man I dealt with. He had a young lady with him who asked if she could use our toilet.' Shannon adds, 'Yes, I remember her. She spotted a picture of Varna on the windowsill, one of the stops on our Black Sea cruise. She said she was born near there.' George quickly Google's Varna and discovers it is a port in Bulgaria. George thanks them for all their help and lovely scones. As before, he tells them he will do everything he can to bring the culprits to justice.

Suffolk's Last Cold War Victim

George drives to his pre-booked hotel in Brough, near Kirkby Stephen just off the A66. He still has a lot of miles to go before he can rest up for the night. As he drives along he keeps thinking about the plight of these poor pensioners. He makes a mutters, 'When I get home I need to check my pension scheme.'

When he has booked in at the hotel he has a light dinner and goes back to his room. He phones Susan, she answers, 'Hello.' He replies, 'Hi darling I just needed to hear your voice. I've heard so many sad stories today what've made me really sad. Now with one word you've cheered me up. How are things there?

'We're both fine thanks for asking. So what's made you so sad? He answers, 'Today I visited four pensioners; each had a heartbreaking story to tell. They've worked hard all their lives, only to be ripped off by a couple of fraudsters. They don't deserve any of this, I just hope my evidence will be good enough to get them arrested and put away for a long time.

Susan knows how to make him feel better, 'Darling I know it's hard but remember to look at the bigger picture. How good will you feel when your efforts get them justice. And if the police can find their money, you'll be a hero in their eyes as well as mine.'

'Once again my little Trojan horse you've managed to blow away the black clouds and give me hope to continue in my task. I'll crack on and give you a call tomorrow, goodnight love.'

Suffolk's Last Cold War Victim

His only solace is the belief that Bannister has been positively identified as Simon Stone and Dumitru as his accomplice. With this positive thought in mind, finally he is able to sleep.

Feeling refreshed and rested, George sets off at 09:00am, for his next appointments in Kendal and Ambleside in the beautiful Lake District, before finishing off in York.

The first call is to Glynne Roberts, a retired Naval Officer and more recently, Hotelier. He lives in a modest, three bedroom detached house in Little Aynam, with views of the River Kent to the front of the property.

Mr Roberts opens the door even before he can ring the doorbell and welcomes George inside. He shows him into a large front room and asks George what he would like to drink George replies, 'A cup of tea would be lovely, thanks.' Mr Roberts picks up a small hand bell and shakes it quite vigorously. This tickles George as he thinks to himself, some habits die hard. A few moments later an elderly lady enters the room. 'A pot of tea and a plate of biscuits please, my dear.' Without saying a word, she simply nods and leaves the room.

As he listens to Mr Roberts giving his account of his dealings with Simon Stone, George begins to sympathise with Bill Murray, the actor in the film 'Groundhog Day' who upon waking has to relive the same things day after day. The lady re-enters the room with the refreshments. Mr Roberts introduces Abigail, his wife to George. 'I'll be in the kitchen if

Suffolk's Last Cold War Victim

you need anything else. I'm sure I'll hear that infernal bell ringing,' she said with a big smile on her face.

Mr Roberts tells George, 'I originally invested £95K in 2014, plus another £35K in 2015. The dividends weren't paid in April 2017, and I've been unable to communicate with Simon Stone Associates since.'

The poor man having worked hard his entire career, was looking forward to his retirement with financial security. Now he and his wife have to downsize, if they want to maintain their thrill-seeking interests; they are both tornado storm chasers. George reassures him he will do everything possible to get justice for him and the other victims of Simon Stone.

His next appointment is in Ambleside, where he is interviewing Mr Philip Wones, another retired Hotelier who lives in a chalet bungalow on the banks of Lake Windermere.

George spots a 'For Sale' sign in the front garden. Mr Wones welcomes George and invites him to join him inside. He follows him down the hallway, into a large living room, though a set of sliding patio doors and onto a large decking area. He sits at a table with soft drinks, glasses and a plate of biscuits. Mr Wones said, 'Glynne Roberts told me you were on the way and will probably be fed up drinking cups of tea.'

He is captivated by the magnificent vista laid out in front of him. River boats full of tourists sail by at regular intervals and the melodic sound of waves lapping on the shore below the decking is the icing on the cake. He makes a note in

Suffolk's Last Cold War Victim

his diary to bring his family to Ambleside for a holiday when the case is finished.

George begins taking notes as he listens to Mr Wones recalling his meeting with Simon Stone in May 2014. His recollections were just as George likes them; short, concise and better still, they were all on a printed spreadsheet.

George said, 'I hope you don't think I'm being nosey but I saw a For Sale board in the front garden.' Mr Wones says, 'Due to the scam and my dire financial situation, I've been left with no option, but to sell up and buy a caravan on a site near my daughter's home in Seascale.'

George is becoming far too comfortable and realises he still has a long drive to his next appointment in York. He politely thanks Mr Wones for his hospitality and evidence.

Back in his car, he looks back through his notes, just in case he has overlooked or forgotten to ask any of his prepared questions. As he reads through the interview he concludes the only differences are the amount of money involved and the dates of their meetings with Simon Stone. The modus operandi was always the same.

George arrives at his next appointment just off Hull Road, close to the University of York Campus East. He is greeted by Mr Donald Masters, a retired Don who worked at York University for 25 years. The names, Don and Masters bring a wry smile to George's face. The story is the same; he makes an investment in April 2015, dividends are paid for the following two years, then nothing in 2017.

Suffolk's Last Cold War Victim

Mr Masters becomes increasingly angry as his story unfolds. Almost in tears he said 'How could I an educated man, fall for such a scam?' he keeps saying it over and over. George is concerned with his host's mental health.

'Don please listen to me, you're not stupid nor are you the only victim of this callous man. So far this week I've interviewed five other victims. I can't divulge the amounts of money they've lost but, I can tell you their previous careers, a Prison Governor, a School Headmaster, a Naval Officer, a Headmistress and an Hotelier. All of them well educated, all had the same ambition as you, to earn a bit more money for their retirement. I'm going to give you the name and phone number of one of the victims, he's the spokesman for the group. Please give him a call and tell him how you are feeling.'

With the interviews now over, he drives to the local Best Western hotel, where he is stopping for the night. He is looking forward to, a good meal and most importantly a bath. As he soaks in the bath, Susan supplies him with all the gossip and events happening in Manor Park.

Just as he is about to go down to dinner, the phone rings. It is Mark Haines. 'George, Mark here. Drop everything you've got planned for Thursday. I need you in my office at 14:00 pm sharp. There've been some major developments following the translations of your recordings. Bring all your files and evidence with you. Your hunch was right; it's so much bigger than just a pension fraud.'

George agrees to bring his evidence and asks Mark if he can send him a transcript of the calls. Mark replies, I'd

Suffolk's Last Cold War Victim

prefer to keep the contents safely under lock and key in my office due to its sensitivity.' 'Ok Mark, I'll be there on Thursday, but I want to interview Geoffrey Hungerford in Suffolk. He was a tremendous help to me on day one.' 'Ok mate, that's your call,' Mark replies.

He spends the rest of the evening cancelling his appointments for Wednesday and Thursday. George is pleased when Colonel Hungerford agrees to see him tomorrow afternoon instead. George hardly sleeps a wink during the night, trying to guess what the translations have revealed, the other crimes, who else is involved and most importantly to him, has he missed something vital to the investigation.

Following a light breakfast of poached eggs on toast and two cups of coffee, he sets off on his long drive to Suffolk.

It's a glorious sunny day in Suffolk as he drives through the narrow, tree lined roads. The kaleidoscope of colours and smells of the wildflowers growing on the roadside helps George relax and take his mind off tomorrow's meeting.

He arrives in the pretty village of Belford around 12:30 pm. He drives around the village to kill a bit of time, before his meeting with Colonel Hungerford.

He's very impressed with the mixture of old and new houses that complement each other. On the main road there is a small number of shops, a Co-op convenience store, a hardware store, a Ford dealership showroom and garage, a flower shop, and a Bookshop/ Art gallery.

Suffolk's Last Cold War Victim

In the village centre, there is a large open green with a children's playground. In the middle he sees a well-maintained cricket wicket with ropes protecting it from the public. Opposite the green stands a war memorial to the villagers killed in conflicts from the Boer war, First and Second World Wars, and more recent conflicts.

The church of St Mary is down a tiny lane 100 yards from the green. George drives past the Colonel's house at the edge of the village, before turning back and parking in the Belford Arms car park.

George spots a number of cars in the village with a sticker in the rear windows with *'Don't Be* a Tosser'. How rude, he thought.

When he gets out of his car in the pub car park, he is close enough to read the sticker properly. It read:

'DON'T BE A TOSSER'
Keep Suffolk Clean
Throw your litter in the bin

This brings a smile to his face, and mutters, 'That's a very clever campaign. Well done BBC Radio Suffolk.'

The Belford Arms looks like a typical village pub. It has a thatched roof, with leaded glass windows. Above the door a large stone lintel has 1894 carved into it. The licensee's name, Mr William Gates, is displayed on a brass plate screwed onto the lintel. He pushes open a large oak panelled door and notices how low the oak beamed ceiling is. For the first time in his life, he is thankful he is not over 6' tall.

Suffolk's Last Cold War Victim

He continues scanning the room and sees a large open fireplace adorned with brass horseshoe figures. A dartboard is in the left-hand corner, the bar is on the opposite side with lots of table and chairs in the middle area.

At the bar he heard another customer say to the person behind the bar say, 'Another pint please Bill.' When the barman finishes serving the customer he asks, 'Yes sir what can I get you?' George asks for a pot of tea and a Ploughman's Lunch off the menu board. The barman, who he assumes is William Gates , gives him a wooden spoon with number 6 on it and says, 'Choose a table, stick this in the sauce bucket and we'll bring your meal and cutlery over. I'll open a tab for you and when you've finished your meal, bring the spoon back to settle your bill.' 'Thank you,' replies George. He selects a table close to a large leather sofa, in front of the large open fireplace.

An elderly gentleman is sitting on the sofa, reading a newspaper; he has a pint mug of beer on a small table in front of him. Looking up, the man speaks to George in a broad Suffolk accent, 'Whoop bor!...Yoo awl roight? George takes a few seconds to work out the question and replies, 'I'm all right thank you.'

'Yoo ent frum row'nd heeya...are yer bor?' the man asks. Once again George waits until he is sure, and replies, 'No I'm from London.'

He's glad this gentleman is not on his list of interviewees; his broad Suffolk accent may have taken him all day to decipher.

Suffolk's Last Cold War Victim

'Wot brung yoo heeya...werk or pleasure?' Getting good at deciphering, George tells him, he has a meeting with Colonel Hungerford this afternoon. 'Aah...the Gen'ral...hee's a good ol booy.'

Just then, the landlord delivers George's meal and drink. The old man goes back to reading his newspaper. A few minutes later he finishes his drink. As he leaves the man says, 'See yer agin bor...cheerio tergither.'

Thinking ahead to tomorrow's meeting in London, George has two options. He mutters, 'Option 1, go home and risk being distracted by the family asking me about my tour or option 2, book into a hotel and work undisturbed, reviewing all my interviews.' He decides the option 2 will be best.

When he finishes the meal, which was delicious, he takes the spoon back to the bar to settle his bill. He asks the landlord if there are any hotels nearby where he can spend the night. 'Why don't you stay here? We do bed and breakfast at a very reasonable rate, and I've a room available for the night,' replies the landlord. George is relieved, 'Excellent, I'll take it thank you.'

He continues, 'Would it be possible to have the room now, so I can freshen up before my meeting this afternoon? And I'd like to book a table for this evening please?' 'Absolutely fine, I'll get your key and please call me Bill,' said the landlord.

The room is spacious, with a large double bed, 2 armchairs, tea/ coffee making facilities, a TV set and an en suite with a bath. Looking out of the window the views of the

Suffolk's Last Cold War Victim

garden are spectacular. A lush green lawn is surrounded on all sides by standard roses, shrubs and bedding plants that are all in bloom. Two six-foot-high privet hedges run down both sides.

The river Deben runs alongside the bottom of the garden. On the other side of the river there are a number of open fields. One has cattle grazing in it; the others have arable crops growing in them. 'This will do nicely,' he mutters himself.

Feeling refreshed, George decides to walk the mile or so to the Colonel's home. He hopes the walk will clear his headache, caused by his lack of sleep and the long drive. It works as he feels much better, when he rings the doorbell.

A tall gentleman opens the door and introduces himself, 'Colonel Geoffrey Hungerford, you must be Mr Mitchell, please come in, we'll go into the dining room. Would you like a drink, tea, coffee or something stronger?' George, wanting to keep a clear head, settles for a cup of tea.

Before they begin the interview George says, 'Colonel Hungerford I'd just like to thank you for the description you gave me last week. With your description I was able to identify a possible suspect.' George shows him a photo of Trevor Bannister and asks, 'Is this the man purporting to be Simon Stone?' As he looks at the photo, Colonel Hungerford's face begins to turn red, 'That's the bastard.' With this confirmation, he goes on to give an almost verbatim detail of their meeting.

Suffolk's Last Cold War Victim

As with the others, the story is the same, only the amounts of money differed. He invested a considerable amount of his pension over three years which produced good annual dividends, but when he wanted to terminate his policies to help fund his son's dire financial situation, he was unable to contact anyone from the company. Groundhog Day all over Again!!!

George thanks his host and tells him, 'I think this concludes our business today. I've a meeting in London tomorrow, where I'll be presenting all my evidence to a panel. Hopefully I'll have some more information for you next week.' With the interview over, he returns to the pub to begin his revision.

For three solid hours, he pores through all his notes and photographs. When he is satisfied, he emails the files and photos to Mark Haines. He feels relieved and confident that he has done everything correctly. It is now 19:30 pm and he is ready for his meal and a couple of drinks to help him sleep tonight.

When he enters the bar he spots the same old gentleman sitting on the sofa. George walks over and said, 'Hello again, my name's George I spoke to you earlier. Can I buy you a drink and join you?' The man replied, 'Whoop George...Moy name's Broy'n...Oy'll plump fer a pint o' Ghoost Ship thankyer kindly.

At the bar, George is about to order Brian's drink, but the name of it has gone completely out of his mind. Thinking quickly, he asks, 'Can I please have a refill for Brian, the same

Suffolk's Last Cold War Victim

for me and take one for you.' Bill replies, 'Many thanks, two pints of Ghost Ship coming up, I'll put it on your room bill. I've just got to change the barrel. You go and sit down and I'll bring them over. The menus are on the table and the specials board is on the back wall.' Looking at the pumps he sees 'Ghost Ship' is brewed by Adnams. He Google's the name and discovers' it's a local Suffolk brewer, based a few miles up the coast in Southwold.

Returning to the sofa, he begins a conversation with Brian. He enjoys listening to and deciphering his Suffolk accent. George asks him how long he has lived in the village.

Brian replies, 'Awl moy loife... Moy ol ma'n'fah were brung up heeya too...Oy still live in their sayme howse.'

The conversation goes back and forth with George asking all the questions. Starting with, 'What do you do for a living? 'Well bor...Oy were a postie in this heeya village...fer noy on forty year...so...Oy could tell a few yarns 'bout them rown'd these heeya parts.' 'Are you married Brian?' 'Oy were, but Oy lorst her ten year agoo.' George said how sorry he is to hear this.

Bill brings the beers over to their table and reminds George he can order his food whenever his is ready. George tells Brian he is staying here tonight and how helpful Bill has been. 'Ol' Moycro...hee's awl roight Oy spooz...hee bought the pub two year agoo...with his compensayshun money...Hee wuz injared inna nexplosion at a chemical plaant.'

George said, 'That's terrible,' before asking, 'Do people call him Micro because his name's Bill Gates of Microsoft

Suffolk's Last Cold War Victim

fame? 'Brian quipped, 'Ho! Thas cause hee's allers troy'n ter give yer short measures.' George nearly chokes on his beer when the penny drops about the reasoning behind his name. 'It's because he always gives you short measures. Priceless' said George repeating Brian's answer.

George is very impressed with his beer. 'That hit the spot, I think I'll have another' he said to Brian. He ends up having two more pints. He said goodbye to Brian before going up to his room for a well-earned rest. 'Adnams Ghost Ship another one for the memory bank.' he said out loud. George sleeps like a baby until his alarm clock wakes him at 7:00 am the next morning.

Suffolk's Last Cold War Victim

Chapter 4

Extra, extra, read all about It!

George opens the curtains and finds himself captivated by the scenery outside. As he stands back, the window resembles a John Constable landscape oil painting in a picture frame. He takes several photos with his camera to show Susan when he gets home.

After a full English breakfast, he settles his dues with Bill, who looks a bit pale and struggling to breathe. George asks 'Are you OK Bill?' Bill nods then utters, 'I get like this sometimes, but I'll be OK in a few minutes, thanks for asking.'

With the bill paid, George sets off for home. He wants a wash and change of clothing before his meeting with Mark this afternoon.

George arrives 15 minutes before the meeting is due to start. As he is shown into the meeting room, he is surprised to find a number of people already seated round the table.

Mark welcomes George and introduces him to everyone in the room. He starts the introductions in a clockwise direction: 'This is my Deputy Editor, Nigel Rolls and my Solicitor, Sophie Patterson. These gentlemen are from the Metropolitan Police. This is Deputy Assistant Commissioner, Richard Long, Detective Chief Inspector, Craig Ferguson, and from the Home Office Border Force, Paul Dorset. Ladies and

Suffolk's Last Cold War Victim

gentlemen, this is George Mitchell, my Investigative Journalist.'

George could not stop himself from saying, 'Wow, this must be one almighty can of worms I've opened up.'

Mark turns to George, 'We've been meeting since 09:00 this morning, listening to the translations and reading your interviews. I'd like you to go through the results of your investigations in chronological order. I've provided everyone with copies of the files you sent me yesterday. Once again I have to say you've done an amazing job. Regardless of whether we can or can't publish the story, a number of bad people will get their comeuppance as a result of this evidence.'

George goes through the evidence starting with the fortuitous manner he, with the help of Colonel Hungerford, was able to identify Trevor Bannister and Ivanka Dumitru. 'I've a number of unanswered questions regarding their relationship. What was Dumitru doing on her visits to the farms and hairdresser salons? Who was the young girl in her car? And what's happened to the money from the pensioners?'

He then gives an account of everyone he has interviewed, the dates and amounts of money each had invested. But most importantly to George, he describes their mental state as a consequence of the fraud.

His presentation takes an hour and twenty minutes. He then takes questions from the panel for another hour.

Suffolk's Last Cold War Victim

The Deputy Assistant Commissioner asks Mark for a short recess. He wants to consult with his team to decide how to proceed with the case. George goes to the canteen for a well-earned tea break. Thirty minutes later, George is asked to return to the meeting room.

Mark turns to Richard Long and asks him to give George an update on their joint agreement. 'Well George, we're all in agreement, due to your tremendous efforts, we're confident we can successfully prosecute a number of very bad, dangerous people, and for that we're extremely grateful.

You're now a main witness, which means you'll be officially interviewed by my colleague DCI Craig Ferguson. I realise you're desperate to read the interpreters' transcripts, but unfortunately this isn't possible at this time. The paper has agreed not to publish the story until our investigations have been completed and arrests have been made.'

Walking round the table, Mark shakes George's hand and thanks him for his work on behalf of the newspaper. 'It would blow your mind, if you knew how your information has helped us to complete the full story. I promise you'll be invited to attend the printing of our story on the eve of it going public. And by the way we're going to double your payment for the scoop.'

As Mark escorts George from the room into the hallway he whispers, 'My good friend Craig Ferguson will take care of you.' George realises he is the Police Officer with a conscience and kind heart. Unbeknown to George, Craig had

Suffolk's Last Cold War Victim

the blessing of the Deputy Assistant Commissioner, Richard Long all along.

Over the next three weeks, George is interviewed five times by DCI Ferguson; they become good friends and met up socially on several occasions. Although George is desperate to find out what the translations have revealed, DCI Ferguson never answers any of his questions on the subject, no matter how he phrases them.

In the end he gives up asking. He is still oblivious on the number of offences his evidence has uncovered. Within a short time he becomes preoccupied working on other investigations.

Finally late on Thursday 1st September 2017, George receives a call from Mark Haines. 'George, early tomorrow morning there'll be a large number of raids across parts of East Anglia.

We've got reporters and photographers ready to record the arrests. Some of these will be used in this Sunday's publication. I still can't go into too much detail, but it's going to be mega.

This is all down to you mate.' After a long pause Mark continues, 'George did you hear that?' George's mouth is so dry he cannot get the words out, and still trying to comprehend what he has just been told.

Finally, he manages to mutter, 'Thanks for letting me know, do you want me to get involved?' Mark replies, 'No mate, you've done enough. You've got to save yourself for the

Suffolk's Last Cold War Victim

trials. Well have a good evening and I'll see you on Saturday evening to present you with a first edition of the paper. Goodnight son.'

On Friday evening George comes in from the garden and notices he has a missed call from Craig Ferguson on his phone. He listens to the voice message. 'Hello George, its Craig, hope you're well? I'm just calling to give you an update on this morning's arrests. We've arrested 31 people for various crimes, and I'm pleased to inform you that your 'Friends' Trevor Bannister and Ivanka Dumitru are among them. They're facing charges of financial fraud, human trafficking/ modern slavery, drug dealing. Dumitru is facing an additional charge of conspiracy to murder.

The Deputy Assistant Commissioner asked me to thank you once again for all your help and cooperation. There's a case of Ghost Ship heading your way as a small thank you. The CPS has indicated the trials will begin early next year; the hard work for you will start then. I'll catch up with you soon mate, goodbye.'

George wants to call him back immediately but he has a strange sense of trepidation. He feels a sensation of pins and needles in his head. He decides to call him back tomorrow. He wants time to think about everything that's happened, and about to happen. Susan notices George is not his usual jolly self. She asks, 'What's wrong darling I can tell something's up?

He replies, 'I've just had a strange feeling of pins and needles in my head. I've never experienced this before. This case is way bigger than I ever imagined. I know you're going to

Suffolk's Last Cold War Victim

say I'm being silly but, I need to tell you something. If anything happens to me, I want you to find someone new to love and cherish as much as you've loved me.' Susan puts her arms around him, 'You're right that's silly. But I love you for thinking that way and I feel that's exactly what you should do as well.'

On 21st November 2017, George receives a letter from the Crown Prosecution Service, informing him the trial will commence on Tuesday 23rd January 2018 at the Old Bailey. He may be called as a witness at anytime in the five weeks allotted for the case. As he reads the letter, George suddenly has the strange feeling of trepidation come over him again. In all the cases he has been involved with, he has never had feelings like this.

Leading up to the trial, George keeps himself busy on other assignments. During one of his regular calls to Craig he confides his feelings to him and asks if these symptoms are normal. Craig replies, 'Of course, in any high-profile case of this kind, it's to be expected, so don't worry mate.' He was glad hearing these words of wisdom from his friend

Suffolk's Last Cold War Victim

Chapter 5

The trial

Of the thirty-one people arrested (a mix of UK and Bulgarian citizens), twelve were released without charge. Another thirteen were tried at Cambridge Magistrates Court in December 2017 for supplying drugs, assisting human trafficking/modern slavery/ prostitution and Grievous Bodily Harm. All thirteen were found guilty on all charges and given prison sentences between three to six years. The Bulgarians will be deported on completion of their sentences.

The trial of the six main defendants will begin on 3rd January 2018. These are the main players controlling the gangs operations, which involved financial fraud, human trafficking/ modern slavery, drug dealing, money laundering and murder. The trial is expected to last up to five weeks.

Two of the defendants Vasil Petrov and Stoyan Ivanor escaped custody whilst on remand in HMP Belmarsh in October 2017. Despite a massive police search, they are still at large. There has been unsubstantiated information they may have been spotted in Bulgaria. They will be tried in their absence.

Suffolk's Last Cold War Victim

In the dock are:

- Trevor Bannister aged 48, British. He ran the pension fraud that financed the human trafficking and drug deals. He also helped Georgieva and Colson in money laundering.
- Penka Georgieva (Aka Ivanka Dumitru) aged 31, Bulgarian. She is the head of the Bulgarian gang in the UK and also the lover of Trevor Bannister. She helped him with the pension fraud and money laundering. She is also charged with human trafficking/ modern slavery, drug dealing and additionally conspiracy to murder.
- Maria Georgieva (Aka Rositsa Borisov) aged 30, Bulgarian. The main organiser and bookkeeper who kept meticulous records of all human trafficking/ modern slavery and drug deals. She is the cousin of Penka Georgieva.
- Vasil Petrov aged 42, Bulgarian. He is second in command to Penka Georgieva and the main gang master. He is in charge of all human trafficking/ modern slavery, drug dealing operations. He is also charged with aiding and abetting a murder.
- Stoyan Ivanor aged 35, Bulgarian. He is Petrov's assistant and is also charged with the same offences. He is the boyfriend of Maria Georgieva.
- Barry Colson aged 63, Scottish. He is the financial brains behind the organisation. He collected the illicit proceeds of the crimes and laundered the monies into numerous offshore accounts.

Suffolk's Last Cold War Victim

Over the next three weeks, the prosecution outlines the part each of the accused played in the gang's operations. The information was obtained from the defendants' computers, phones, and documents seized on the day they were arrested. The records found at Maria Georgieva's address proved how far and wide their criminal enterprise covered. The most damning information is the recordings and photographs provided by George and the Police surveillances leading up to the arrests.

Matthew Love the Barrister for the prosecution opens the trial and explains how it all began. In the summer of 2011 Penka Georgieva (aka Dumitru) and her cousin Maria Georgieva (aka Borisov) arrived in the UK using false passports and aliases. They obtained employment picking fruit and vegetables on farms in and around the Ely area.

They realised they could make extra money, using their family connections to supply the farms with cheap labour from Bulgaria and other eastern European countries.

For the rest of that summer they scouted farms and food processing factories that used seasonal casual workers. The information they gathered was sent back to the family in Bulgaria. The family began assembling a small team to join the girls in the UK.

Vasil Petrov and Stoyan Ivanor are the first to arrive. Petrov is used to managing and controlling an itinerant workforce. Ivanor was Vasil's assistant and boyfriend of Maria Georgieva. Over the next few months, a number of others followed. These were mainly the hired muscle men, charged with maintaining discipline amongst the workers.

In the first year their enterprise was successful and very profitable. Over the next two years the gang expanded their operations further afield in the surrounding area. They also begin supplying workers for other businesses; beauty therapy salons nail bars, prostitution and drug dealing.

At a Young Farmers' fundraiser held in November 2012, Penka Georgieva is introduced to Trevor Bannister by his friend Barry Colson. Over dinner, Bannister told her about his pension business and his ambitions for the future. She was very interested listening to him talking about financial investments, something she thought may be of use to her current enterprises. They agree to meet up again the following week to discuss her financial investment opportunities.

Colson is pleased his introduction had gone well, as he had information on both of them. He knew Bannister was having something of a mid-life crisis and dreamed of making a lot of money, to help him start a new life somewhere warm and far away from the UK. He also knew that (in certain nefarious circles) Georgieva was making a lot of money for herself and may need some help managing it.

During their subsequent meetings, a physical attraction began to grow between them. Their talks were now filled with things they would like to do, once they had made enough money to start a new life together.

The prosecution produced evidence, found at the office of Colson, which showed in December 2012 Bannister,

Suffolk's Last Cold War Victim

Georgieva and Colson created a company named Simon Stone Associates. At first it was a cover to enable money laundering of the proceeds from the supply of labour.

Over the next few months they add to their portfolio by supplying labour to hairdressers and nail bars. Bannister saw an opportunity to boost the funds, so with the cooperation of Colson, he added a Pension Investment company to Simon Stone Associates portfolio. They began to entice pensioners to invest in this company. Simon Stone Associates banked their customers' investment funds and paid them dividends each year, by using their own investment money.

Soon after the gang added drug dealing and prostitution, to their ever-growing list of dubious businesses. These businesses were increasingly left to junior members of the gang to run. The main players were still raking in a lot of cash each month.

By this time Bannister and Georgieva had become lovers and were finalising their plans to move to Dubai under new aliases. Colson's share of the proceeds would have enabled him to retire very comfortably, as he recorded in his diary, details that were very helpful to the prosecution.

In February 2017, having made enough money for their new life together, they decide to shut down all Simon Stone Associates operations. A total of 226 pensioners were known to have been a victim of the pension fraud.

The funds were transferred into various offshore investments in the Cayman Islands and Swiss bank accounts by Colson. George listens to the proceedings in a side room.

Suffolk's Last Cold War Victim

He is shocked that a small number of people inflicted all this misery on so many people.

George is called to give his evidence on Thursday of the second week of the trial; his testimony in the witness box lasted two days. The court listened to George's recordings of Georgieva's in Starbucks and The Barley Mow pub in Wisbech. They heard the original recordings in English and translations when she spoke in Bulgarian.

She is heard talking to members of the gang and her family in Bulgaria. She tells them of her and Bannister's plans, to extradite themselves and their money from the UK.

The photographs of the documents taken in Starbucks on 28th July 2017 are also damning, as it provides bank account names, numbers and the amount of cash in each of them.

George and the court are shown a photograph of a young man by the prosecuting barrister. He asks if he recognises the man in the picture. He replies, 'Yes, I do. I saw him working in a field. I gave him a can of drink. I remember him becoming very agitated when he spotted the Range Rover driven by the woman I believed to be Ivanka Dumitru.'

The court is shown more photos of the man, who is named as Stefan Batinkov. In one he is seen lying in a drainage ditch, just off the B1145 near Gayton. In another he is on a pathologists table, bloodied, bruised and a bullet shaped hole in the middle of his forehead.

Suffolk's Last Cold War Victim

George feels lightheaded and physically sick; the judge asked him if he wants a short break. After taking a sip of water, he said he is ok to continue. The court then hears a recording of Georgieva giving specific instructions for Stefan Batinkov to be terminated immediately. Georgieva has information he is about to go to the police and claim asylum. The judge thanks George for his evidence, and he is allowed to stand down.

On Monday of the third week, DCI Craig Ferguson begins giving his evidence on the police surveillance operations, leading up to the arrests of the gang on 2nd September 2017. On Friday the case for the prosecution concluded their evidence.

Over the next four days, the defence lawyers try valiantly to defend those in the dock and the other two defendants in their absence. Because the prosecution's evidence is so strong (especially George's) their tactics were to try and get as much of the prosecution's evidence deemed inadmissible. The judge the Right Honourable Ms Sandra Higgins however was having none of it.

The jury retired on Tuesday 30th January to consider the evidence and returned on Friday 2nd February to give their verdicts. The judge asked the foreperson of the jury if they have reached a decision on the charges against all the defendants. She replied they had.

As the judge reads out each defendant's name she asks her to answer guilty or not guilty to each individual charge against them. Over the next 10 minutes the Jury Chairperson

Suffolk's Last Cold War Victim

answers guilty to every one of the six defendant's charges. The judge thanks the jury and witnesses for their cooperation in the trial. She remanded all the defendants into custody until sentencing on Wednesday 14th February.

Outside the court, the Deputy Assistant Commissioner Richard Long and DCI Craig Ferguson, gives a press statement to the mass of assembled press reporters. Standing close by with the biggest smile on his face is Mark Haines.

DAC Long begins, 'I'd like to thank everyone involved in bringing this cruel, sadistic, murderous gang, and the case against them, to a successful conclusion. Special thanks must be given to George Mitchell for his work in the investigation.' George's stomach turns over as he listens to his comments. He experiences the same feeling of trepidation he had when the arrests were made.

DCI Craig Ferguson taking questions from the press was asked if the monies have been recovered. He answers, 'Not only has most of the money been recovered, there is a good chance the pensioners will receive a substantial percentage of their investments back.'

George phones Susan to inform her of the verdict and to let her know the following weekend he will be taking her, Jason and his girlfriend Sarah Mann on a short break to Ambleside in the Lake District. They will be staying in Phil Wones bungalow, now he does not have to sell it. She is thrilled with the news. 'Finally, we'll be having you all to ourselves for a few days.'

Suffolk's Last Cold War Victim

Mark Haines invites all the main players back to his office for a celebratory drink. This time George has to respectfully turn him down, as all he wants is to get back home to his wife and son.

Suffolk's Last Cold War Victim

Chapter 6

What's going on?

Wednesday 14th February George takes a cup of tea up to Susan, who is still in bed. He tells her, 'This time next week my little Trojan horse, we'll be on our way to the Lakes.' After kissing her goodbye, he sets off to his office. He did not sleep very well during the night, as he still has an uneasy feeling of apprehension that something bad is about to happen.

Outside the weather mirrors his mood, dark, overcast and cold. He goes in early to finish off some work, before he heads to the Old Bailey to hear the sentencing of the gang members.

At 10:00am he begins his journey to the court, arriving 45 minutes later. Craig Ferguson and Mark Haines are already in the waiting room. Sentencing is due to begin at 11:15am, but news comes through that there will be a short delay. This is due to an incident involving the prison vans en route to the court.

Craig is not unduly worried, as he has seen this a few times before. Traffic congestion in the city is usually to blame. After 10 minutes Craig's phone rings, as he answers the call George notices Craig's face has turned as white as a ghost. 'Please excuse me gents, police business, I just need to take this call outside.' With that he leaves the room shutting the door behind him.

Suffolk's Last Cold War Victim

George keeps pacing about the room unable to sit down or standstill. Mark is getting annoyed, 'For goodness sake George, sit down. You're going to wear the carpet out.'

Fifteen minutes later, Craig and a number of armed police officers enter and quickly usher George and Mark out of the room. They are escorted through a set of doors towards the back of the court. George asks, 'Craig what's going on.' Craig replies, 'I'll explain everything I know when we're safely in the police van that's waiting for us in the rear courtyard.'

The van races out of the courtyard with the men safely on board. Craig tells them about the information he received earlier. 'Police HQ has informed me there've been two major incidents involving two of the three prison vans, bringing the defendants to court for sentencing. One is carrying Bannister the other has Penka and Maria Georgieva inside. It appears both vans have been ambushed simultaneously, and the prisoners have all escaped. A number of prison guards have been seriously injured. For your protection, we're on the way to a high security police station, until we can get more information.'

Both men are initially speechless, until Mark asks Craig about the sentencing. Craig informs them the judge has decided to pass sentence on Colson in person; he is travelling in another van, the remaining five in their absence.

Suddenly George shouts out, 'What about my wife and son? Can I give them a call and warn them to go somewhere safe?' Craig replies, 'I'll do better than that; I'll send a police car round to collect them.' Craig rings police HQ and gives

Suffolk's Last Cold War Victim

them George's address in Manor Park. George knows he cannot relax until they are both safe. The men arrive at the Police Station twenty minutes later and are shown into an interview room on the 6th floor.

George knew something bad was going to happen today. It would have been bad enough that three criminals have escaped, but not in a million years could he have imagined the news Craig is about to tell him.

One hour later Craig enters the room with tears running down his face. Struggling to speak, Craig manages to utter, 'George, please take a seat. I'm so sorry to inform you the officers sent to collect your family discovered the front door ajar. When they entered your home, god I don't how to tell you...' George panicking asks, 'Tell me what Craig, what is it.' Craig continues, 'They...they found Susan and Jason's bodies in the kitchen. They had both been shot and I have to tell you, they're both deceased.'

After a short pause George jumps up screaming, 'No, no, what's happening here? I need to see them. Please Craig, take me to them.' Craig replies, 'Sorry mate I can't do that, your home's now a major crime scene. I promise you, we'll find the bastards responsible for this atrocity.'

Another senior officer DCC Clive Whiting enters the room. He said, 'George, we're all so sorry for your loss and we'll do everything possible to find the killers. Craig can I have a word please?'

As they step outside the room he said, 'We believe the attacks on the prison vans and the murders of George's family

Suffolk's Last Cold War Victim

may have been planned and executed by members of the gang still at large.

We found a typed message 'You're next' left in the house. For his safety I need you to persuade him to enter a witness protection scheme? We don't believe Mark's under threat at this time, but we'll provide armed officers at his home and offices until further notice. Thanks mate.'

Returning to the room, he sees George crying like a baby in Mark's arms. While he is composing himself, Craig speaks to Mark, telling him he is free to continue with his business albeit under police protection for a few days.

Turning to George, who is drying his tears, he said, 'For your protection I want you to go into a witness protection scheme until we apprehend the people who did this.

This means in the short term you'll be taken to a safe house. Long term, you might have to use an assumed name, a new identity and live in a new location. I'm afraid we must get you out of here and into a safe house as soon as possible.'

Turning to Mark Craig said, 'Sorry mate, but we've got to get moving. I'll arrange a car to take you wherever you want to go.'

Mark gives George a big hug; saying, 'I'm so sorry for how things have turned out. I promise the paper will pay for all your expenses. We'll do everything in our power to assist in the capture of everyone involved in these despicable crimes.'

Suffolk's Last Cold War Victim

George's thoughts are of Susan and Jason. Were they tortured? What were their last thoughts? Why didn't God protect them?

Craig asks George to follow him into another room, where they will be alone with more privacy. Craig tells him, 'We can talk through any questions you have and it's a quiet place for us to pray for them.' George's first question is, 'When can I see my family so I can say a prayer with them.' Craig knows how much it means to his friend said he will arrange it as soon as practically possible, bearing in mind his safety, which is now his main concern.

After saying a prayer for Susan and Jason, George asks Craig his thoughts on what he should do now. Craig said, 'I know this sounds callous, but we can't go back in time. We have to move forward. If I were in your position, I'd start to make plans for the future. You need to create an alter ego for yourself, a new look, new name and a new location to start again.' George knows his friend is just being cruel to be kind. Deep down he knows he is right.

George stands up, walks round the table and hugs Craig tightly without saying a word. After a few minutes he said, 'Craig, you truly are a good friend. You're absolutely right I need to focus on the future. After listening to those poor pensioner's stories, it made me realise how easy it is for depression to set in following a traumatic event. I don't know everything I want to do yet, but I do know where I want to live, the Suffolk village of Belford.'

Suffolk's Last Cold War Victim

Later that evening, George is taken to a safe house in Chelmsford, Essex. Here he can at last grieve for his family. Two days later Craig, true to his word, manages to arrange a meeting for George to see Susan and Jason for one last time.

They both looked so beautiful and at peace. The mortuary staff did a wonderful job covering up their wounds, these images helped to put his mind at rest, as he spoke and prayed with them both.

George is given a few newspapers, but cannot bear to read them so soon after his terrible ordeal. For the first few days all the national newspaper's headlines, are awash with reports of the ambushes and murders. Now only one newspaper kept it on their front page all week, that paper was 'Everyday News,' the sister paper of 'World of News'.

Mark gives him a call around midday to check on his welfare. He asks if he has heard the judge's sentencing. He tells Mark about the conversation he had with Craig yesterday and how he is focusing on the future and no, he had not heard.

Mark said, 'The sentences are as follows;

- Trevor Bannister 25 Years imprisonment.
- Penka Georgieva (Aka Ivanka Dumitru) Life imprisonment with a minimum 30-year term.
- Maria Georgieva (Aka Rositsa Borisov) 25 years imprisonment.
- Vasil Petrov Life imprisonment with a minimum 30-year term.
- Stoyan Ivanor 15 Years imprisonment.

Suffolk's Last Cold War Victim

- Barry Colson 25 Years imprisonment.

Listen mate let me know if there's anything you need, or if you just want someone to talk to. Give me a call anytime, day or night.' George thanks him for the call and promises he'll take him up on his kind offer.

A few minutes after they finished the call, George cannot remember any of the sentences handed down by the judge. It takes all his courage to pick up one of the newspapers and begin reading the reports. He is glad he made this decision, as he knows this small step is just the beginning of the marathon journey on the road to his new life.

At the end of the first week, Craig visits George to brief him on the police investigations. The police obtained some CCTV footage from a car dash cam. The images show one of the vans stopped at a set of red traffic lights. The van driver is clearly seen lowering his window and throwing a cigarette butt out. The image of the man has been positively identified as Vasil Petrov, a member of the gang, who escaped from Belmarsh prison whilst on remand in October 2017.

Both vans were found burnt out with no useful forensics. The bullets found at your house matched a bullet used to kill Stefan Batinkov, so we know the gun and the gang were involved in both crimes. Changing the subject have you spoken to Mark?'

He replies, 'Yes, I spoke to him yesterday. A couple of days ago I told him I wanted to relocate to Belford. He phoned to tell me he'd found a cottage for sale in the village and wanted me to take a look on the estate agents link. It was

Suffolk's Last Cold War Victim

perfect, better than I could ever have imagined, I said I loved it. You could've knocked me over with a feather when he said "Leave it with me I'll put an offer in for you tomorrow morning. Don't worry about the money I'll pay for it, you can pay me back when your house has been sold. Don't worry about the legal expenses I told you we'll cover those."

Craig, 'It's about time things are starting to go your way. Now you've got a location have you had any more thoughts on the other elements? George answers excitingly, 'I have, my alias will be ASHLEY MOORE, Ashley was my dad's Christian name and Moore was my mum's maiden name. I'm going to let my hair grow longer and dye it black and I'm going to wear a pair of glasses.

Craig, 'I see you've been busy.' George thanks Craig for all his help and support, but most importantly, his friendship. He said, 'Craig, I want to start my new life as soon as possible. I've no ties here now and I don't want to be reminded everyday of what I've lost. Can I do this?' Craig replies, 'I'll check and let you know next week if that's ok?' George nods.

Craig is pleased his friend is starting to focus on the future, rather than spiralling into the abyss of depression. He asks George how he manages to be so positive. He replies looking him straight in the face, 'I may have lost my family physically, but their spirits are still with me. I talk to them regularly and hopefully once the funeral is over, they'll finally be able to rest in peace.'

11:30 am. Tuesday 27th February. George is writing in his note book when the phone rings, he answers, 'HI Mark

Suffolk's Last Cold War Victim

how's things with you? I really liked the cottage in Belford. I viewed the photos and I think I'd be really happy there.' Mark says, 'That's good as I've just received a call from the estate agent. He told me the vendor has accepted my offer for the cottage. The good news is I got it for ten grand less that the asking price. I also agreed a short rental lease from the 16th April until contracts are exchanged and completed. You can move in any time after that date.

George shrills, 'That's brilliant news I'm so pleased, thanks mate. Now I can finally start to plan my new life. Will it be ok to let Craig know? Mark answers, 'Of course, he'll need time to notify the witness protection team and other authorities concerned in your case.

'I'll give him a call right away. I can't wait to get out of here and start meeting people again. On the subject of meeting people, the police forwarded me all my post from my old house. One was a lovely letter from Glynne Roberts one of the pensioners I interviewed. He and his wife have invited me to spend a couple of weeks with them in April. I'll ask Craig if this'll be ok when I phone him. I really hope they'll agree it.

Mark said, I'm sure Craig will authorise it for you. Well lots to do, it's great to hear you being positive again. I'll phone again soon, bye mate.

George ends the call and phones Craig right away. When he answers George said, 'Hi Craig, have you got a few minutes to talk? 'Yes mate fill your boots.'

George adds, 'I've just finished a call from Mark; he's given me some great news. He's bought me a cottage in

Suffolk's Last Cold War Victim

Belford and I can move in from the 16th April. I've also been invited to spend a couple of weeks in Kendal with Glynne and Kim Roberts. I just wanted to run it past you to see if there'd be any objections.

Craig asks, 'That's great news I'm really pleased for you. Mr Roberts wasn't he was one of the victims? George answers, 'Yes he was. He sent me a lovely letter saying how sorry they were for my misfortunes and offered to look after me as a thank you for helping them.'

Craig, 'Right I'll make a few calls to see what I can do. It'll take a few days to arrange. I'll call you when I've some news. Bye mate.'

12:30 pm. 8th March. The doorbell rings, George checks the spy hole and sees Craig standing outside. He opens the door

'Hi Craig come in, this is a pleasant surprise.' He enters and said, 'Hello George I was going to phone but I thought I'd surprise you.' George Answers 'That sounds intriguing.'

Craig continues, 'I can confirm the funerals will be held on Sunday 1st April, strictly for family and very close friends only. The cemetery will be protected by the Met's armed police. Now I've got some really good news for you. These are for you Mr Ashley Moore.'

Craig hands George a large envelope, As George opens the envelope he pulls out the contents, as Craig explains what they are. 'This is your new passport, driving licence, and car insurance... George interrupts, 'But I haven't got a car.'

Suffolk's Last Cold War Victim

Craig said, 'Yes you do, have a look outside.' George walks over to window and looks out. He sees a 2017 registered black Toyota Yaris. Turning to Craig he does not know whether to laugh or cry. Regaining his composure he utters, 'Wow! How much do I owe you?'

Craig said, 'You don't owe me anything this is all Mark's doing. He bought it with the advanced payment for your new book. You can use it on your trip to Kendal and the journey to Belford.'

George is puzzled, 'Book, what book, I'm not writing a book.' Then the penny drops, 'I've just realised what you said, that's Mark all over... 'Another short pause, 'You mean my trips been authorised! That's fantastic news.'

Craig says, 'There are however two small caveats. Firstly from this moment on you're to be known as Ashley Moore. Secondly you'll have to call Cumbrian police every morning telling them where you'll be going.'

Ashley close to tears says, 'How can I ever repay you both for all your help? When I'm in my new home I'd like you and Mark to spend the weekend with me so I can treat you to a meal and a few beers in the Belford Arms.'

Craig looks out of the window. 'Well I must be going my lifts just turned up. Here are the car keys. I'd prefer it if you stayed in until your drive to Kendal. It'll give your hair more time to grow and get it dyed.'

Ashley goes to open the door, 'That's the least I can do and anyway I've got a book to write. Actually an idea's just

Suffolk's Last Cold War Victim

come to me, I'll write about a man starting a new life in another part of the country after a major tragedy.'

    Craig walks down the path and calls out, 'That'll work as long as you don't make it too personal.'

Suffolk's Last Cold War Victim

Chapter 7

New beginnings

On Monday 2nd April with the funeral finally over, George is able to contemplate his life. He has a new name and address away from the city, not far in mileage terms, but light years away from his previous life.

He has a blank canvas on which to paint a new future for himself, starting with a new look. His hair is several inches longer and dyed black. The new look was completed with a pair of thick rimmed glasses; the lenses are just for show, as he has a very good eyesight.

Just leaving the safe house in Chelmsford and driving to Kendal gives him a feeling of freedom again, something that helps him both physically and mentally.

When he arrives in Kendal Ashley is welcomed warmly by his hosts. Ashley has already made Glynne aware of the threats to his life; he did not want to put them in danger too. Glynne tells him in no uncertain terms, 'As long as you're under my roof, you'll be totally safe and secure. So just relax and have a good time.'

His hosts know when to engage in conversation and when to leave him alone with his own thoughts. Ashley goes for daily walks around Kendal and the surrounding area, plus day trips further afield.

Suffolk's Last Cold War Victim

One day he drives to Bowness-on-Windermere, taking a return boat trip to Ambleside. As it is a beautiful sunny day with only a light breeze, he decides to sit on the open upper deck. The views are fantastic, with the surrounding mountains keeping a fatherly eye on the smaller rolling hills. As he looks out to the views on shoreline, the captain announces over the loudspeaker, 'Ladies and gentlemen in the next five minutes we'll be arriving in Ambleside.' He remembers interviewing Phil Wones in a beautiful lakeside Chalet bungalow in Ambleside.

His mood takes a turn for the worse as he recalls the booking he made for his family on the very weekend after they were murdered. His eyes fill with tears as the bungalow appears approximately 100 yards away.

As the boat sails closer, now immediately opposite the property less than 50 yards away, he sees a pretty, blonde haired woman and teenage boy, also blonde, walk through a pair of open patio doors onto the decking. The woman has one arm around the boy and he can see the smiles on their faces. They both wave in his direction. Ashley stands bolt upright and says out loud, 'Oh my God, Susan, Jason is that you?' He also begins waving back. As the boat sails on, the pair are still smiling as they turn and disappear back into the bungalow.

For the first time in weeks his gloom is lifted, and he feels a warm feeling running through his body, believing his family are starting a new journey of their own. The tears are still raining down his face, but weirdly, these are now tears of relief and happiness. In that moment, nothing or no one

Suffolk's Last Cold War Victim

would be able to convince him, that they (his family) were not real; no one!

On Friday of the first week, he takes a bus ride to Coniston Water, and once again decides to take a boat trip on the lake. During the trip, the guide provides an interesting historical talk on Donald Campbell and his world record speed attempt on 4th January 1967. The boat stops over the spot where his boat 'Bluebird', rose into the air and turned over a number of times before breaking up and sinking, taking the great man to his watery grave.

On Monday of the second week, having discovered a liking for the Lakes, he decides to walk around Grasmere. Setting off from Ambleside, he walks along the main road to the lake. On this visit he keeps mainly to the edge of the shoreline walking in a clockwise direction. When he reaches Grasmere, the halfway point of the walk, he sits down for a welcome meal and drink in the local public house.

Feeling refreshed he begins his journey back to Ambleside, but there is still one more place he wants to visit; Dove Cottage the home of William Wordsworth, the poet responsible for 'I wandered lonely as a cloud' and 'The Prelude'.

The following day, on the advice of Glynne Roberts, he sets out to climb Blencathra, an 868m (2848 foot) mountain. The weather could not have been better for his maiden climb; there is not a cloud in the sky. Glynne tells him, 'If you like a challenge take the route over the famous Sharp Edge ridge line.' Glynne was right; it was a challenge and certainly not

Suffolk's Last Cold War Victim

one for the faint hearted. The sights on offer when he reaches the top are breathtaking. He sits looking around, taking in the sights for well over an hour, before making the descent back to his starting point.

After he has given his guests an account of his trip, he goes up to his room. For the first time since the tragedy, he manages to sleep right through the night.

The next morning, Ashley makes a few phone calls. The first is to Craig Ferguson, to make sure his move to Belford is still on track. Craig confirmed all is well with no outstanding police issues. He also contacted Mark Haines who is dealing with his house purchase, he has more good news. The monies have been deposited with the solicitors, so there should be no delays once the contracts have been exchanged. 'I'll be in the village on Monday to meet you and hand over the keys. Then you, my friend can introduce me to a pint of your favourite ale.'

On the last day, Ashley treats his guests to a top-notch meal, as a thank you for their amazing hospitality. He makes a promise to keep in touch and hopes next time they meet, he can use his proper name again.

Monday 16th April is a momentous day for Ashley. This is the day he is truly starting a new life. Although the journey to Suffolk took five hours he still feels refreshed and in good spirits.

Driving through the pretty Suffolk roads brings back memories of the first time he visited Belford. The smells of the spring flowers and blossom from the trees were sublime; in

Suffolk's Last Cold War Victim

this moment he knows he made the right decision to move here.

Ashley arrived on the village outskirts just after two o'clock. Driving along the main street he catches sight of the Belford Arms pub. He mutters to himself, 'See you shortly', remembering he has promised to take Mark for a meal there.

His Satnav system announces, 'In 100 yards turn left'. Following the instruction, he drives into Old Oak Lane. He continues for another 150 yards and hears, 'You have reached your destination'. He stops the car outside a large cottage. He recognises it from the estate agent's brochure and video. He remembers walking past the cottage, on the way to Colonel Hungerford's home and seeing a 'for sale' sign in the front garden.

Mark waves as he walks down the driveway from the front door. He uses a remote control to open a large pair of automatic wooden gates. Seeing Mark and his new home Ashley is so excited, he promptly stalls the car as he is about to pull into the driveway.

Mark opens the car door and helps Ashley out of the car. After a welcoming man hug, Mark hands his friend a large bunch of keys. He says, 'There you go George, I mean Ashley. These are yours. Let me show you round your new home. We'll start in the kitchen, I've made a brew and some sandwiches, just in case you haven't had anything to eat or drink en route.'

Ashley replies, 'Thanks mate, but first, can you direct me to the bathroom, I don't want any floods on my first day.'

Suffolk's Last Cold War Victim

He reappears looking a lot less flushed and says, 'That's better. Now you can show me round my new home and garden, then I'll treat you to something special in the Belford Arms.'

Mark informs him, 'I've had security specialists install a state-of-the-art intruder alarm system covering the cottage and garden. Anyone entering the grounds will be detected and activate an alarm. This alarm sends images to your mobile phone so you can check their identity.'

The cottage decor is fairly modern considering its age, it was built in 1948. Two years ago the previous owner had the interior modernised. It now has all the mod cons you would expect to find in a newly renovated home.

Mark begins the tour upstairs showing him round the three bedrooms, two with en suites. Ashley is pleased his request for all bedrooms, to have new beds and linen fitted has been completed. Downstairs comprises a large kitchen, utility room, dining room, lounge that looks out into the garden, bathroom and a separate toilet. On the right-hand side of the cottage is a detached double garage.

The garden is very similar to the view he saw from the pub's bedroom window on his first visit. Through a gate at the bottom of the garden he spots the River Deben. From this point he estimates it is approx. ten feet wide, with fields on the other side. Moving closer he sees a small rowing boat moored up on a jetty. Before he can ask, Mark said, 'That's yours as well mate. The oars are in the garage, along with the rest of your belongings from your old house.' Seeing Ashley's

Suffolk's Last Cold War Victim

eyes being to well up he said, 'Are we going for that drink or what?'

Following a short walk to the pub, Ashley is anxious to see if his new looks will fool Bill Gates, the landlord. He orders two pints of 'Ghost Ship' and is relieved Bill did not recognise him. They take a seat on the sofa near the fire to catch up on things. Mark asks Ashley for his mobile phone, he needs to programme it to receive the security alerts.

Ashley tells Mark all about the holiday with the Roberts' and how much he enjoyed the experience. He asks Mark if he believes in ghosts. Mark, not quite knowing where this is going replies, 'Yes, I do. There're things that happen, or people see things that can't always be easily explained away. I'll tell you one Ghost I do believe in, it's this beer.' He did not want to ask him why, so quickly changes the subject.

Mark continues, 'I asked Craig for an update on the police investigations. He said, although the whereabouts of the gang are still unknown, they're confident they're still in the country.

The police believe they still have a substantial amount of cash stashed away, which they'll have take with them when they eventually try to escape. They're also confident all the money they put in their overseas accounts has been accounted for.' Ashley asks, 'How can they be so sure?' Mark said, 'Barry Colson has agreed to cooperate fully with the fraud squad and provide them with additional information, they weren't previously aware of in return for more favourable prison conditions.'

Suffolk's Last Cold War Victim

They spend the rest of the afternoon talking and drinking. At six o'clock they order their meals and another round of drinks. Ashley is a bit disappointed Brian, the old gentleman he met the last time he visited, was not in the pub. He wanted to introduce him to Mark, so he could hear Brian's Suffolk dialect and see if he could understand what Brian is saying.

After his long drive this morning and the boozy session in the pub, Ashley is ready for his bed. Mark agreed to stay with him on the first night, to make sure his friend was OK and make sure all the security systems are working correctly. As Mark enters the front garden, Ashley's mobile phone begins to vibrate and buzz; when he presses the accept icon on the phone, a very clear image of Mark appears on the screen. The system appears to be working correctly, much to their relief.

The next morning Ashley wakes and goes down to the kitchen to make a cup of coffee for himself and his guest. He is surprised to find Mark already sitting at the kitchen table. 'How did you sleep?' he asks Mark. He replies, 'Not very well I'm afraid. The silence was deafening, and then the birds started singing at the crack of dawn. I can't wait to get back to the city noise. How did you sleep?' Ashley explains, 'I've been sleeping exceptionally well since the funeral. Every night before laying my head down, I say a prayer for them both, this helps me greatly.'

Over breakfast, Mark asks Ashley what his plans are for the future and can he help in anyway. Ashley tells him he plans to write a book about the past year's events, to help him fully understand the tragedy. Mark, with his editor hat on,

Suffolk's Last Cold War Victim

agrees this is an excellent idea and asks if his paper can run the story, when it is safe to do so. He did not expect, nor did he receive an answer.

After breakfast Mark said he should be making his way home and wishes his friend well, promising to visit him again in August.

When Ashley closed the front door, he became aware of how alone he is. No family, no close friends and no one to share his new life with. After a big sigh he gives himself a good talking to. 'Pull yourself together, get out there, make new friends and start your new life, beginning today.'

He decides to knock on the doors of his nearest neighbours and introduce himself to them. The ones who answered seemed very friendly as they welcome him to the village.

As he is walking along the road towards the village green, he spots an elderly gentleman walking towards him. Ashley recognises Colonel Hungerford; they both said 'Good morning' to each other. A few seconds later, Ashley hears the Colonel's voice. 'George, is that you?' Turning round, Ashley replies, 'Colonel, yes, it's me. Please may I speak to you in private, I've a lot I need to get off my chest. I know I'll have your complete trust, when you hear my predicament.'

He answers, 'Of course you can, come with me. We're so sorry to hear the terrible news regarding your family and we've been following the story in the press.' They turn round and they begin walking back to his house, arriving there ten minutes later.

Suffolk's Last Cold War Victim

When they enter the house Ashley is led into the lounge, which the Colonel believed was vacant. He is surprised to see his son sitting on a fireside chair, reading a newspaper. 'Peter, what are you still doing here? Haven't you got some gardening work to do?' he barked at the poor man, who immediately rose and left the room apologising, 'Yes father, I'm going right away.'

The Colonel shakes his head and mutters, 'I don't know what's wrong with that boy. He's a 58-year-old man, who is still living with his parents.' Turning his attention back to Ashley he says, 'Right young man, let's have it, what's your problem?' For the next twenty minutes, Ashley gives the Colonel a full breakdown of the events that brought him back to the village, with a new identity and appearance.

He listens intently to Ashley's story before he reaches out and shakes his hand and said, 'Hello Ashley, my name's Colonel Geoffrey Hungerford, please call me Geoffrey. If there's anything I can do for you and I mean anything, please don't be afraid to ask. If you like, we can meet up again this evening in the Belford Arms. I'll introduce you to a few of the villagers at our bridge match.'

Ashley feels much better knowing he has a new trusted friend and neighbour. 'How did you know it was me?' he asks. The Colonel replies, 'During my army career, I was trained to observe and recognise a person's appearance and voice. Can you recall the first time we spoke? I gave you a description of Bannister. I remember you saying that it was a long time ago, but I was right wasn't I? I recognised you immediately. If that's

Suffolk's Last Cold War Victim

all, I hope to see you this evening. These are my home and mobile telephone numbers.'

Ashley gives the Colonel his mobile number and thanks him for listening to his problems. 'I'll definitely be there this evening.'

The rest of the morning is spent walking around getting used to the layout of the village and buying some groceries. After a light lunch, Ashley decides to have a short cat nap. He only wakes when his mobile phone rings; he is stunned to discover he has been asleep for three hours.

The phone call is from Craig, who just wants to check if everything is going OK. Ashley says, 'Thanks for calling; everything's going well so far. I've got to admit I gave Colonel Hungerford the full story when he recognised me earlier.' Craig is pleased another pair of eyes is looking out for him. He finished by saying how he was looking forward to his visit on 28th April.

Suffolk's Last Cold War Victim

Chapter 8

The new kid in town

In the evening Ashley takes a relaxing stroll to the pub, as he enters he is greeted by Colonel Hungerford. He introduces him to two men and a woman seated at a table playing bridge.

'Everyone, this is my good friend Ashley Moore, the son of one of my former army colleagues. He's just moved to the village and I'm pleased to say, he's agreed to honour our local tradition of buying all the pensioners in the pub a drink.' The Colonel looks around and says, 'Luckily for him, we're the only ones in here at the moment.' The woman rounds on the Colonel saying, 'How dare you sir. I'm not a pensioner, but I'll still accept a drink.'

He continues, 'Ashley, this lovely lady is Mrs Nicola Scott. She's the Conservative councillor for East Suffolk and also chairs the local planning committee. Next to her is Perry Lakeman; he used to be the landlord of this fine establishment. We always get him to order our drinks, so Micro over there doesn't try to give us short measures and finally, Adie Dale, a retired car salesman.'

Ashley greets them all with a handshake before he introduces himself, 'Welcome everyone as the Colonel said my name is Ashley Moore. I'm an ex-civil servant attached to the

Suffolk's Last Cold War Victim

foreign office, and that was all I'm allowed to say on the matter.' He sees the Colonel trying to stifle a laugh.

He asks them what they would like to drink. Ashley gives Perry some money as goes to the bar to order their drinks. The new boy pulls up a chair to join them. By the end of the evening he has a good understanding of the game of bridge. At the end of the evening he said goodbye to the group and tells them, he looks forward to seeing them again very soon.

Early the next morning he is once again woken by the ringing of his mobile phone. This time it has a different ring tone. As soon as he presses the security app button, he sees it's the postman delivering his mail through the front door letter box. He looks at his clock; it shows 06:25 am, his alarm is set for 07:30 am. He wants to go back to sleep but the sun, streaming through his window wins the battle with the alarm clock, to get him out of bed.

He is reassured the system is working correctly. He writes on his 'To Do' list; buy a new mailbox and fit it next to the front gate.

Over breakfast he begins thinking of things he would like to do today. He decides to go for a row along the river in his boat. As he goes to the garage to collect the oars, he spots a familiar figure sitting on his garden bench, looking out over the river.

He checks his phone to see if he has missed a security alarm message, when he was in the garage. The alarm did not detect his visitor. Ashley knows the alarm activated earlier

Suffolk's Last Cold War Victim

when the postman entered the front garden. The only other way to gain access to his property is through dense hedges either side his neighbour's gardens, or by someone using a boat on the river. There are no footpaths on his side of the river; there is however one on the opposite side close to the fields.

The man asks 'Heow do George...Yoo awl roight bor?' Walking across the lawn towards him, Ashley said, 'Hello Brian. Yes, I'm fine thanks. I'm so pleased to see you. I've been in the pub a couple of times and was disappointed you weren't in there. But how did you know I'd moved here and how did you get into the garden?'

Brian replied, 'Fust O' vawl...when Oy were a young'n...Oy use ter goo scrump'n heeya...so Oy knew heow ter git in 'n' owt without bee'n fow'nd owt...an' there ent nuthen that goo on in this heeya village withowt me know'n about ut...Specially a new furrener... Doont aask me heow Oy knew ut were yoo.'

Ashley has missed the guessing game with Brian. He manages to work out most of the phrases, but one word, furrener, stumped him. Brian gives him the definition, someone born outside of Suffolk.

Ashley knows the front security is working correctly and he also knows there are no other boats moored up on the jetty. Brian's clothes are dry so he did not wade across the river. The only plausible explanation is he must have come through one of his neighbours' hedges.

Suffolk's Last Cold War Victim

To be on the safe side, Ashley makes a phone call to the security company's fault line to report a possible failure. The security companies operatory tells him they have an engineer working nearby and said they will get him to call round within the next hour.

Ashley is in a quandary, should he tell him the truth or risk Brian calling him George in the presence of others? He decides to let it run for a while until he can explain things properly.

Brian asks, if he minded him being there. Ashley replies, 'Absolutely not, in fact I'm really pleased to see you. I need a new project to keep me busy for couple of weeks. I thought I'd write a novel about a 'Furrener', see I'm learning, who moves to a Suffolk village.

I'd be grateful if you can give me a brief history of the village and its inhabitants, past and present. Of course, I'll change all the names and locations.' Brian replies, 'Course Oy will...Oy ken tell yer things that'll turn yer guts insoide owt...Oy ent a goss'p moind, now goo'n git a pen an' a scrap a payper.'

'Brian, would you like a drink when I come back?' He is surprised when he declines the offer of a glass of 'Ghoost' Ship. Ashley asks, 'When the engineer's finished his checks would you like to go for a ride in my boat?'

'Not ser loikly,' he replies. 'Oy hent got gills or wings...so yer 'on't git me on the warter or up in a playne either.'

Suffolk's Last Cold War Victim

Sitting comfortably, Brian admits his knowledge of Belford only goes back as far as his grandparents' time. He has knowledge of the surrounding villages Pettistree, Bredfield, Ufford and Rendlesham. He was their postman for many years, until his retirement in 2005.

Ashley said, 'That's fine as my village will be fictional and I'm more interested in the villagers' personalities. I know, let's begin with you. Tell me all about yourself, warts and all.'

Brian takes a while before answering, 'Yoo'll git more'n 'at...toyme Oy've done jor'n...Oy were born in moy parents' hoom in 1940...an' Oy've bin livv'n heeya ever since.

Ashley said, 'Sorry Brian, you said, "Time I've done jor'n" what does jor'n mean?'

Brian replies, 'Cood blaast mee! Oy hent half gotta job on heeya...larn'n yoo Suffolk...jor'n means talk'n...Oy need to git yoo Suffolkated soo'n possible...the darts ternoight up the Aarms...a cuppla three o' moy owd schoolmaytes'll be play'n...look owt fer Smiffy 'n' Sharpie...jest yoo lissen to em jor'n...if yoo hear suffen yoo doon't unnerstaand...jest aask mee.' Ashley asks if he will be there too. He said he has other things to do this evening.

He decides to take his voice recorder with him this evening and then play it back to Brian tomorrow.

Listening intently to Brian telling his life story Ashley is desperately trying to keep up writing his notes on Brian's recollections.

Suffolk's Last Cold War Victim

Brian's parents Allen and Agatha Damant had three children, twin daughters Brenda and Nancy, Brian followed them five years later. His father and grandfather were both herdsmen, working on the local farm. His parents lived in a tied cottage, where all the children were born and raised.

They all went to the local village school until they were eleven. Then they had to travel to Wickham Market high school, over three miles away.

Both sisters married when they were eighteen and moved out of the village. Brenda trained to be a nurse; she lives in Ipswich where she worked until her retirement at the age of sixty-five.

Nancy was the academic one of the family, so it was no surprise when she qualified as a teacher and began a lifetime teaching in Woodbridge. Brian has always been proud of his twin sisters' achievements. Although they are in their eighties, both are still happy and healthy.

Between and after the two world wars an increasing number of military airfields were built in Suffolk. As a result the village began to expand with an influx of air force and army personnel. Major Gary Wales, the largest landowner in the fifties and sixties, made an enormous about of money selling his farms and land around the village to the government.

The Major used the money to purchase a large estate in the Scottish Highlands, for his retirement home. He was an extremely benevolent man. His parting gift to his loyal employees was a large sum of money, to be divided equally

Suffolk's Last Cold War Victim

between them all. To the tenants who lived in the ten tied cottages in the village, he presented them with the keys and deeds of these properties.

When Brian married Maggie, a 'Furrener' in 1962, they lived in his parents' cottage. This worked well as money was tight when they first got wed, and then many years later, they were there to help care for his elderly parents.

His parents both died in 1993; his father went first, followed six months later by his mother. In their wills, Brian was left the cottage, his sisters shared the life insurance pay-outs and other monies left in their bank accounts.

Brian and Maggie as a result of her fertility problems were never blessed with children. Their marriage had been happy and loving until her death in 2008. She was 63 when her car was hit by a lorry that jack-knifed on the A140 while on the way to see her sister in Norfolk. She died at the scene of the accident.

Just then Ashley's mobile begins ringing; it is the security engineer who just entered the front garden. He said, 'Excuse me for one minute, whilst I let the engineer in.' When he returns to the garden, after letting the visitor in, he is surprised to find Brian is nowhere to be seen.

Thirty minutes later, the engineer tells him he was unable to find any faults in the system. He wonders how on earth did Brian avoid being detected, and where has he disappeared to?

Suffolk's Last Cold War Victim

He is itching to go on his rowing trip. He settles himself in the boat before he sets off rowing downstream. He passes a number of homes on his side of the river, before being surrounded by fields on either side. After thirty minutes he decides to moor up by a large tree for a short rest. He lays back, pulls his cap over his face and closes his eyes.

Forty minutes later he wakes from a deep sleep, wondering where on earth he is. After recovering his bearings, he begins rowing back to his cottage. During the trip he only sees one other person, walking his dog along the footpath. He wonders how many people he would have seen if he had been rowing along the River Roding, close to his former home. Although he thinks of his family every day, it has been a long time since his thoughts are of Manor Park.

Suffolk's Last Cold War Victim

Chapter 9

The darts match

Following a long soak in the bath to ease his aching muscles, he gets dressed and goes to the pub for his dinner. He orders a Ploughman's Lunch, which goes down well with a lovely cold pint of Ghost Ship. After the meal he moves to a table closer to the dart board in readiness for the match.

The pub quickly fills with diners and darts players. Ashley looks round to see if he recognises anyone. He is pleased when Colonel Hungerford and his son Peter walk in. At the bar the Colonel spots Ashley and mimes, 'Do you want a drink.' Ashley replies with a thumb up, also miming, 'Yes please, a Ghost Ship.'

They walk over to Ashley's table, the Colonel says, 'Hello Ashley, you've met my son Peter before, haven't you? Is it ok to join you?' He replies, 'Of course and thanks for the drink'. Reaching over, he shakes hands with Peter and introduces himself properly.

The Colonel asks, 'Are you here for the darts?' Ashley replies, 'Not really, I'm writing a book about a fictional Suffolk village, and I need to learn the local dialect. My new friend told me to come here tonight and listen to the men jor'n.' 'Well, I see your friend has given you a good start' said the Colonel.

Suffolk's Last Cold War Victim

Ashley begins asking Peter about his life in the village. He seemed on edge and not very sociable, answering questions with as few words as possible. Ashley assumes his father's presence may have a bearing on his tense demeanour.

While Peter is at the bar, his father tells him, 'Because of his alcohol and gambling addictions, Peter's wife in Manchester has thrown him out. With no money, no job and nowhere to live, his only option was to move back here and live with us. His mum spoils him rotten; I on the other hand, keep pushing him to keep himself busy. I've got to admit he's trying very hard to control both of his addictions. I haven't told him yet, but I'm very proud of his efforts.' Ashley wanted to say, 'If he was my son, I'd praise him up to the hilts.' But as it is another family's matter, he decides to keep quiet.

During their talks he discovers Peter has been doing gardening work for some of Belford and the surrounding villages' pensioners. After the fraud Peter went out of his way to get more customers, to help with his parents' finances.

'Is Brian, the retired Postman, one of his customers?' asks Ashley. 'He most certainly is, but nobody has seen him for the last two to three weeks. Peter overheard someone saying he'd gone to visit an old friend.'

Ashley did not think any more about it as he assumes Brian has only recently returned without Peter knowing he is back.

Just as Peter returns with the drinks, the first match begins. The opponents this evening are The Fox, from the

Suffolk's Last Cold War Victim

nearby village of Melbridge. The match consists of twelve, best of three 501games.

    Ashley looks around to see if can find Brian's two school friends. Sitting on a table in front he sees two elderly men. Could they be Smiffy and Sharpie? 'Colonel, do you know the names of those two men sitting in front of us?' he asks. The Colonel replies, 'The one on the left is John Smith and the other is Trevor Sharp. They're both in the team tonight.'

    As the first match begins, Ashley places his recording device, as close as he can to the duo on the table. He understands most of their conversation, but some of the sayings go right over his head. He becomes so engrossed listening to them that he has no idea which team is winning.

    Halfway through the match the Colonel decides to call it a night, leaving Peter alone with Ashley. Peter's demeanour changed immediately when his father walked out of the door. He asks Ashley all about his move, where he came from and if he has a family. Ashley feels really bad he has to tell him so many lies. Peter remains aloof when Ashley asks questions on his history.

    They talk continue talking for another forty minutes until, Peter immediately decides to call it a day when Ashley asks him a question about Brian. He does not say goodbye or even finish his drink, he just quickly walks out.

    Ashley decides to introduce himself to Brian's friends. He said, 'Excuse me, my name's Ashley I'm new to the village. A mutual friend of ours Brian, told me to speak to you guys.

Suffolk's Last Cold War Victim

He wants you to help me to become Suffolkated.' They both shake his hand and welcome him to the village.

John Smith said, 'Howd yoo haard...whoile Oy give this heeya young'n a hooly good sole'n.' He goes off to play against a younger opponent. Trevor Sharp looked at Ashley's glazed expression and interprets John's words. 'You wait here whilst I give this youngster a good thrashing.' This brings a big smile to Ashley's face. He asks, 'How come you can speak near perfect English?' Trevor whispers, 'I haven't always lived in the village. I moved away for couple of years because of my job. I learnt to speak differently so my workmates would understand what I was saying. Please don't let the others know, as they'll disown me.'

John's game did not last long he was beaten in both games. He walks back to his seat with a face like thunder. 'Oy Lett'm win cause his muther's watch'n.' Trevor, reverts to his native dialect says, 'Yoo're sorft as loights yoo are... yoo duzzy bugger.'

After the games finish, Ashley thanks the two men for their help this evening and looks forward to seeing them again. He also looks forward to replaying the recording, to see how much of it he has understood. As he is about to leave John tells him, 'That looks hooly bad oover Will's Muther's...Do yoo Moind heow yoo goo.' As he walks home, he tries to work out John's last sentence. It made no sense, except the hooly bad bit. It is the last thing on his mind when he falls asleep and the first thing when he wakes in the morning. He cannot wait until he can ask Brian for an interpretation.

Suffolk's Last Cold War Victim

Chapter 10

The little bugger's brigade

The alarm clock begins ringing at 07:30 am. The alarm is not needed today as Ashley has been awake since 06:00 am listening to the rain beating on the windows. He is thinking how much he had enjoyed the previous evening in the pub.

The main characters for his book are beginning to formulate in his mind. He picks up his laptop and begins typing his thoughts on the characters so far.

- The prodigal son –Trevor Sharp
- The oracle –Brian Damant
- The strict father - Colonel Hungerford
- The tough talker, with a heart of gold- John Smith

He concludes he needs to include some female characters on his list before he chooses who will be the lead character in the novel.

He realises why he is feeling hungry when he looks at the clock and sees it is 09:30 am. After washing and dressing, he goes downstairs for some breakfast. As he reaches the bottom of the stairs, he sees the silhouette of a figure through the front door glass panel. Panicking, he quickly checks his mobile phone to see if he missed an alarm message, when he was in the bathroom.

There is no message and he had not heard the doorbell ring either. Instinctively he shouts out, 'Who's there?' Not

Suffolk's Last Cold War Victim

really expecting a reply, he is surprised and relieved when he hears a familiar voice say 'Thas Broy'n...hurry up George 'n' let mee in...thas a hellava chuck'n ut dow'n owt heeya.'

Feeling secure again he unlocks the door and lets his friend into the hallway. Although it's raining steadily outside, Brian appears to be totally dry. Ashley thinks the only plausible reason for it, is that he has been sheltering under the front porch for a while.

'Sorry Brian, I didn't hear you ring the bell, please come in. Would you like a drink and something to eat?' Brian replies, 'Oi'm awl roight thank yer koindly...did you jor with moy ol' muckers?' Ashley said he had, and they were both very nice and entertaining. He adds he has recorded a lot of new words and phrases that he couldn't work out their meanings.

Brian says, 'Well bor...less git a-goon...givvus yer fust one.' Ashley plays the one that has been bothering him all-night. "That looks hooly bad oover Will's Muthers". Brian laughed, trying very hard to speak slowly, as he gives an explanation of the phrase. 'I think a storm is on its way, and hee wuz roight an'awl.'

The next phrase, "Yoo're sorft as loights yoo are" he explains 'You are as soft as lights you are, or someone that can easily be led or used. Lights are animal lungs that are very soft to the touch.' Ashley is very surprised to hear Brian talk without his broad Suffolk accent, he asks, 'How did learn to speak like that?' Brian replies 'That's a yarn for another time.'

Suffolk's Last Cold War Victim

Ashley asks Brian if he can continue with this posh voice as there are so many questions he wants to get through today. He begins by asking how long he had known John and Trevor. He is pleased he asked him to talk this way as Brian keeps him entertained for the next two hours.

Brian said, 'I've known Smiffy and Sharpie since we were nippers. My earliest recollections are of us playing together on a farm, whilst our mothers were busy fruit or pea picking. Our highlight was being taken to and from the fields on the back of a trailer pulled by the farmer's tractor.

We enjoyed our adventures in the nearby woods, building dens where we'd hideout. We also loved swimming and fishing in the river Deben. We were proud we leant to swim. Boys who couldn't swim were the ones with tide marks around their necks.'

Ashley asks, 'Sorry Brian can you explain what a tide mark is? Brian said. 'Most families only had a bath once a week, usually on a Sunday evening in a galvanized tub in front of the fire. The rest of the week they washed in the sink, only cleaning their hands and face. As the week went on, a thin line would appear round their necks, just like seaweed left on the beach at high tide. As we were always in the water, we rarely suffered from it.

We all went to the same school in Belford, before moving up to Wickham Market high school when we older. At least this school had changing rooms, with running water and indoor toilets. There was no excuse for kids to have tide marks there.

Suffolk's Last Cold War Victim

We always stuck together, helping one another if anyone picked on us. The local kids called us 'The little bugger's brigade'. The only antisocial thing we ever did was to go scrumping. Before you ask scrumping is pinching fruit from other people's gardens.

When we were thirteen, we got a Saturday job selling paraffin round the village for Kev's Cars. We took it in turns to pull a trolley loaded with large barrels full of fuel. In the sixties paraffin was used for heating, lighting homes and also preventing the outside toilet plumbing from freezing up. Most customers brought they cans out and watched us fill a gallon measuring can, before transferring it to their cans.

Some customers left their cans to be filled and the money in their back gardens. We took these cans to the trolley, filled the measuring jug, when we emptied it into the customer's cans, we left a small amount in the jug. We poured this into a five gallon barrel which we owned. When there was enough in the barrel we used this to fill customers' cans, keeping the money as a bonus for us at the end of the day. Oy weren't sorft', as I always pulled the trolley on the last leg, because every gallon we sold made the trolley lighter.

We all left school at fifteen without any qualifications, but it didn't take us long to find jobs. Sharpie worked for Kevin Beardmore, owner of Kev's Cars, the garage on the High Street. He promised him an apprenticeship with two provisos. Firstly he had to pass a three-month trial, which he did with flying colours. Secondly, if he attempted to have any physical relations with Kevin's seventeen-year-old daughter Shirley, he would be sacked and run out of the village forever.

Suffolk's Last Cold War Victim

Smiffy beat a number of other school leavers to a get job in the local Co-op convenience store, just over the road from the garage.

I went to work in my uncle, George Debman, in his butchers' shop in the nearby village of Bredfield. I didn't enjoy butchery very much, so when a vacancy came up in the local Post Office, I spoke to my uncle about my feelings. Uncle George thanked me for my honesty and gave me a glowing reference, which helped me secure the position of office boy.

When we turned sixteen, our attention turned to the opposite sex. There was always a conveyor belt of new girls coming and going in the village. This was a result of the number of new homes being built, and the turnover of military personnel from the nearby airfields living here.

Sharpie, was the best at attracting the prettiest girls, he got the nickname 'Mr Whippy.' Smiffy was the last one to lose his virginity. He's really fussy, he normally only went for tall, dark or black-haired girls, even though he's fairly short. He wasn't the sharpest tool in the box either. On one occasion at the school hall youth club, he danced and bought drinks all night for a girl with a promiscuous reputation, from the neighbouring village. When he asked if he could walk her home, she told him not to bother as she was on her cycle, she meant she was menstruating. The silly bugger said 'Tha's alroight; I'll run alongside yer.'

I wasn't bothered though, I'd go with any girl who showed an interest in me.' At this point Ashley asks, 'Excuse

Suffolk's Last Cold War Victim

me, Brian, why did you call Trevor Mr Whippy? Was it because he's cool and tasty?'

Brian replies, 'We didn't, it was the gals, he suffered from premature ejaculation. He didn't last long when he was touched by the gals, so he'd whip it in, whip it out and wipe it.'

Ashley gives out a massive laugh when he works out the poor man's predicament. With tears of laughter running down his face, he thought it a good time to have a tea break. But once again, Brian turns down the offer of a drink.

When they resume Brian continues, 'When we turned seventeen we all worried that any day, a letter may arrive in the post informing one or all us we'd been called up for National Service. The day finally arrived for one of us, that person was Sharpie. He was absolutely gutted as he was going to be away from his mates and his new girlfriend, Shirley Beardmore for at least a year.

We all think it was Kev's doing when he found out he was courting his daughter, he must've written a letter to the authorities. As it happened, Sharpie enjoyed his two years in the army. He was selected to join a specially trained unit to protect high ranking officers and their staff, in the event of a nuclear attack on any of Suffolk's airfields.

This is where he met an ambitious officer, Major Geoffrey Hungerford. Because of his local knowledge, Major Hungerford always kept a good look out for him. When he was de-mobbed, he resumed his apprenticeship and courtship with Shirley, this time with Kev's blessing. Both me and Smiffy noticed he din't talk proper no more.'

Suffolk's Last Cold War Victim

Ashley asks, 'Do you know what Sharpie and his army friends did to protect these people in the event of a nuclear attack.' Brian replies 'I remember Sharpie telling me, all around Suffolk there's a number of small shelters, built deep underground. In the event of a nuclear alert their job was to transport key personnel to the shelters which would provide protection for them for up to thirty days.

Roight...thas mee done fer t'day...if yoo want ter learn more...jest yoo toon inter Radioo Suffolk this arternoon...Lesley Dolph'n's on with Chaarlie Haylock...yoo'll learn moor frum him. 'If you go to the local book shop buy some of Mr Haylock's books, I can recommend 'SLOIGHTLY ON TH' HUH!'

Before he leaves, Ashley says, 'Thanks for coming round I've learnt a lot today. At least the rains stopped. By the way Brian do you have a telephone number I can call you on?' He replies 'Oy had one, but Oy've lawst ut.'

As Ashley opens the front door for Brian his phone begins to ring. He quickly runs back to the kitchen to pick it up. He hears Brian say 'Cheerio tergither', by the time he gets back to the front door, which takes no more than ten seconds, Brian is nowhere to be seen. He keeps doing that, but how?

The call is from Craig, 'Hi Ashley I'm sorry due to work commitments I won't be able to visit on 28th April, but I can make the following day.' Ashley said yes immediately, as he knows he has nothing booked in his diary for this or any other date.

Suffolk's Last Cold War Victim

Craig asks, 'How are things going there?' Ashley said 'Everything's going better than I ever dreamt it could. Changing the subject is there any news on the gang's whereabouts? Craig replies, 'Despite some promising leads, nothing has proved productive at the moment. Hopefully when I come to see you, there'll be something good to report.' They continue speaking for another ten minutes before saying their goodbyes.

Over lunch, Ashley switches on the radio and tunes in to Radio Suffolk to listen to Lesley Dolphin's afternoon show. He didn't have to wait long before listening to Charlie Haylock's distinctive Suffolk dialect. He is very informative and amusing. Ashley cannot wait to tell Brian how much he enjoyed the show. When Charlie asked the show's listeners to send him their questions on all things Suffolk, he made a note of his e-mail address. He mutters to himself, 'This will come in handy, if I get stuck on a word or phrase when writing my novel.

Suffolk's Last Cold War Victim

Chapter 11

Kindred spirits

As the weather begins to brighten up, Ashley decides to go for a walk to clear his mind and get some exercise in the fresh air. He walks down the main road to check out the businesses where the 'little bugger's brigade' worked. The only one that has changed its name is Kev's cars. It is now a Ford Dealership, owned by Stephen D'eath. The fuel pumps have been removed and a small showroom stands in its place.

Walking towards the village green, he hears the familiar sound of a church organ playing his favourite hymn, 'All things bright and beautiful'. The music is like a magnet attracting him towards its source.

It suddenly dawns on him, this is the first time he's been in a church since his family's funeral service in April. He believes God is trying to bring him back into the fold. It feels good as he walks through the doors of St. Mary's. He makes his way quietly down the aisle to the front pews, immediately behind the organ player, and sits down to listen to the music.

The woman playing the organ was oblivious to her audience, until she finishes playing and Ashley said, 'That's my favourite hymn.'

He makes her jump; she had not heard him come in. She turns round and sees a stranger looking back at her. She

Suffolk's Last Cold War Victim

says, 'I'm sorry I didn't hear you come in.' Ashley replies, 'No I'm sorry I startled you. I was walking past, when I heard you playing and I couldn't resist seeing who was playing the organ so beautifully. My name's Ashley, I moved to the village on Monday.' Laura replies, 'Pleased to meet you Ashley, my name's Laura, Laura Archibald. Welcome to our village.'

Laura leaves the organ and comes down to shake his hand. This is the first time in nine weeks he has been alone talking to a female.

He guesses she is in her early to mid-forties; roughly the same height as him, with long black hair, tied up in a ponytail.

He asks, 'Do you live in the village?' She replies, 'Yes, I live in Beech Road, just around the corner from the Belford Alms. Where have you moved to?'

'I've moved into a lovely cottage in Old Oak Lane', he replied.

'Yes, I think I know the one you mean; I remember seeing the 'For Sale' board in the garden. Number 14, wasn't it? Has your family settled in OK?' she asks.

This simple question knocks him for six for a few seconds. He quickly regains his composure, wondering if he should tell her the full story or a fabricated version. He does not want to tell lies in a church so decides to tell her basic facts.

Suffolk's Last Cold War Victim

He says, 'Unfortunately, my family were both killed in a tragic incident a few months ago. I decided to leave the city to live in the countryside, so here I am.'

She is shocked with this news. She walks over to him and holds out both arms before gently interlocking her hands with his and said, 'I'm so sorry for your sad loss. I too know how it feels to lose a loved one. I lost my husband Philip in a tragic accident four years ago. Shall we sit down and say a prayer for them?'

He replies, 'Yes please, I'd like that very much.' Ashley thanks Laura for her lovely prayer. He told her she has rekindled his faith in God, which has been on the back burner since his family's demise.

Leaving the church they continue to talk about the village and its inhabitants. She tells him she is a teacher at the local primary school and plays the organ at the weekend church services.

As he listens to her talking about the villagers, he kept thinking 'She reminds me of a female Brian. Before they know it, they arrive at her front gate. He asks if he can attend this weekend's church service, so he can listen to her playing again. She laughs and tells him, 'I'd be very disappointed if you're not there.'

'That's a date then,' he replies, before realising his face is going red and sounding like a teenager. He hears her laughing as she walks down her garden path.

Suffolk's Last Cold War Victim

Walking past the pub, he thinks to himself, should I go in and have a quick pint or not, he decides not. There are so many things, names and places he wants to put down on paper before he forgets them.

The best thing to come out of today came in the form of a church organist, schoolteacher with a very pleasant personality. She will be the first female character to feature in his book.

When he gets home all he wants for his evening meal is a plate of beans on toast. When he finishes his meal he grabs his notebook and pen, and settles down in front of the television on his sofa.

Over the next four hours he switches between watching the telly and jotting down bullet points for his novel. He did not realise how tired he is until he sees what he has added to his list

- Peter Hungerford, Hidden secrets
- Laura Archibald, Kind, talented, must find out more.

He mutters, 'Not much for a journalist. Tomorrow I must go shopping for food and a new mailbox.

With that he turns off the telly, checks the doors and windows are secure and makes his way upstairs to bed. As usual he speaks to Susan and Jason, telling them all the things he has been up to today. Just as he is about to drift off, he thought he heard Susan say, 'Laura seems very nice, we like her.'

Suffolk's Last Cold War Victim

Chapter 12

That place north of Diss

Ashley is still in a deep sleep when his mobile phone rings and vibrates. He guesses correctly the culprit is the postman. When the new mailbox has been installed, he hopes his alarm clock is the only thing that wakes him in the morning.

Over breakfast Ashley Google's 'Mailboxes' and sees one he likes. It can accommodate large letters, small parcels and newspapers. He measured the location earlier, so he knows it will fit nicely in the spot beside the front gate.

He set off for Ipswich a little after 10: am, hoping to miss the rush hour traffic. He has only driven a few hundred yards when he sees Brian walking towards him. He stops the car and winds down the window. 'Hello Brian, were you coming to see me?' he asks.

'Oy woz…but Oy see Yoo're goo'n off somewhere,' he replied. Ashley continues, 'I'm going to Ipswich to do a bit of shopping. Why don't you come with me? I could do with your local knowledge.' 'Awl roight Oy'll goo…Oy hen't gotta lot on t'day…yoo ken aask some more things for yer book.'

Ashley is a bit concerned watching Brian trying unsuccessfully to open the passenger door. He jumps out,

Suffolk's Last Cold War Victim

walks round and opens the door for him. Brian explains 'Oy've bin sufferin' frum artheroytus 'n Oy caan't grip things.'

After getting Brian into the car and securing his seat belt, he returns and drives away.

Brian asks, 'Wot yer after bor?' Ashley replies, 'I'm looking for a new mailbox to go next to my front gates. You're the expert on this subject being an ex-postman. Where's the best place to buy one in Ipswich?

Brian tells him about a second-hand sales yard on the northern outskirts of Ipswich, which sells this type of thing. 'If they hent got any...wee'll hatter goo row'nd tow'n...to a few haardware shops.'

'OK, let's do that. If all else fails I've seen one I like in Screwfix.' said Ashley.

As they begin the journey Ashley wants to discover more about Brian's wife, so he asks him how and where they met.

'Well George...at wer loike this bor...In layte summer o' noineteen sixty...a load o' the ol' booys frum the village went on a cooch trip ter play in a daart tornament in Grayte Yaarm'th fer the weekend...Oy'll tell yer suffen George...that oopen'd our oyes...Them ol' Norfolk booys were rumm'ns...but the gals were suffen diffrunt.'

Ashley quickly butts in. 'Hold hard Brian (he's pleased he used this phrase) can you say that again, there's a couple of things I didn't quite understand?' Brian's a bit annoyed but understands he's talking to a furrener replies, 'I suppose I'll

Suffolk's Last Cold War Victim

have to speak with my posh voice today, with you interrupting me every couple of minutes, I'll never finish this yarn before dark.

As I said, in the late summer of 1960, we went on a coach trip to Great Yarmouth to play in a darts tournament. The Belford Arms team won the Ipswich and district darts league and were asked to represent the league in the Norfolk and Suffolk tournament.

We arrived on a Friday evening before the tournament and booked into a guest house in Great Yarmouth. When we'd booked in, me, Smiffy, Sharpie and two other friends decided to find the nearest pub, before going on to a dance hall.

This was the first time many of us, except Sharpie, had left the safety of our beloved Suffolk. The noises and bright lights were mesmerising to us vulnerable youngsters.

The first dance hall we went to was full of teddy boys, all dressed in smart suits which attracted the prettiest girls. We felt out of place and handicapped by our attire. Although we were all dressed in smart suits, we couldn't compete with these guys in the girl pulling stakes.

We left when it was obvious we weren't getting anywhere and went to another dance hall further away from the seafront. This one was a little smaller but there were more girls than boys, which helped our chances to find someone to dance with and more, if you get my drift.

I spotted a pretty gal with long black hair, wearing a pink and black dress, sitting on a chair next to the dance floor.

Suffolk's Last Cold War Victim

She smiled at me every time we made eye contact. I had a pint of beer and a whisky chaser for some Dutch courage, before going over to ask her for a dance. As I approached her, I stood on one of my shoelaces that had come undone and went arse over tit, landing up on my back with my head almost under her dress. Her friends were calling me all kinds of things from "dirty pervert", "sex maniac" etc.

I got up and walked out of the hall as fast as I could. When I was outside I took the shoe off and threw it against a wall as hard as I could. It bounced off the wall into the road just as a bus drove by and ran over it, just my bloody luck.

I retrieved the shoe and sat on the kerb to fit it back on. That's when I heard a woman laughing; as I turned round I saw it was the gal from the dance hall. She'd followed me out and saw the whole shoe throwing episode. She said, "That's the funniest thing I've seen in weeks, you should ignore the comments of my friends. Would you like to come back in and dance with me or we could go for a walk?"

I told her I never ever want to go back in there again and agreed we should go for walk instead. She told me her name was Maggie and she came from that place north of Diss.'

Ashley just about manages to stop laughing out loud, but he can't stop the tears of laughter welling up in his eyes after hearing this story. He asks, 'This place north of Diss. Where is it, and how come you can speak without your normal Suffolk brogue?'

Suffolk's Last Cold War Victim

Ashley knows Brian is obviously irked by his questions when his broad Suffolk brogue returns. 'Cood blast...yoo doon't half aask a lotta sorft stuff...Yoo'll hatter werk ut owt yerself...Oy'll give yerra cloo...Budgies are wot they call their football tea'm...If yoo say ut in moy cumpnee...yoo 'on't see mee ever agin...Secondly...Oy'll tell yer layter heow Oy learnt ter jor posh.'

Having got this off his chest he continues, 'Maggie held my hand as we walked along the promenade in the dark. There wasn't a cloud in the sky and no wind, so it was very quiet, except the clip clopping of my bloody damaged shoe.

We kept walking for about a mile, before taking a seat in one of the promenade shelters. The moon's reflection on the North Sea made it a really romantic setting.

We talked about many things, our families, jobs, likes, dislikes and our homes. As it was getting late I asked if I could walk her back to her B&B, which was about a hundred yards from where I was staying. I was really happy when she said OK; she also agreed to meet me the next day at the darts tournament.

When we arrived at her digs, I said goodbye and told her I was looking forward to seeing her again tomorrow. I'd only gone a few yards when I felt someone tugging on my coat. As I turned around, Maggie threw her arms around my neck and kissed me on the lips.

I was gobsmacked. The smell of her scent, the touch of her skin, the taste of her lips and when I looked into her eyes, I knew this woman was going to be my wife.'

Suffolk's Last Cold War Victim

The tears begin to well up in Brian's eyes. Ashley knows he has to keep quiet until Brian wants to talk again. He did not have to wait long, before he heard him say, 'Take the next left into that yard sign posted Whitmore Relics.'

The yard is like an Aladdin's cave full of all manner of garden furniture, ornaments and recycled phone boxes. Unfortunately there are no mailboxes.

So it was on to the next location, a Hardware shop, located just off the 1214 in Kesgrave, near Ipswich.

Brian said, 'I reckon it'll be quicker to go over the Orwell Bridge to get there.' Driving over the bridge Ashley tells Brian how very picturesque it is. On the left hand side, he sees the Port of Ipswich. On the right the River Orwell winds its way to the estuary and the Port of Felixstowe, the tall booms of its cranes are clearly visible.

Entering the store, he is disappointed to find that although the store sold mailboxes, they were all too small for his needs. He decides to go on-line and order the one he had seen earlier in the Screwfix catalogue.

The only store with one in stock in the Ipswich area is at Martlesham Heath. He orders one on click and collect, available in one hour's time. This is ideal as there's a large Tesco store nearby. He can get some shopping, while waiting for it to be processed and it's on the way home.

When they arrived in the Tesco car park, Ashley asks Brian if he needs anything from the store, or did he want to

Suffolk's Last Cold War Victim

come in for something to eat and drink in the cafe. He replies, 'Oi'm OK...thank yer koindly.'

With the shopping and mailbox collected, they begin the journey home. Ashley prompts Brian to continue the story of the darts tournament.

He begins where he left off earlier. 'After we'd finished kissing, we agreed to meet up again for breakfast in a café a couple of doors from my B&B.

When I met up with the boys, one of them was missing, Ollie Fosker at forty-three, was the oldest on this trip. When I asked where he was, Smiffy said, "You're not the only one that got lucky tonight." As it happened, lucky isn't the word I would've used now I know the facts.

Two months later, his wife went to her doctor saying she's having unusual discharges from down below. After some tests, the doctor informed her she's suffering from Gonorrhoea.

She knew it must have been Ollie that gave it to her. When she confronted him he admitted he was responsible. He told her he must have caught it on the darts trip. One night he got so drunk he couldn't remember anything about the night or who he'd been with.

He thought she was going to kick him out, but she didn't, his punishment was no more sex from that moment on. I asked Ollie how he felt about it. He said he wasn't bothered, as she was a good cook and kept the house clean. And now he doesn't have to give her at least four organisms

Suffolk's Last Cold War Victim

every time they have sex.' Ashley interrupts, 'Don't you mean orgasms?' 'No, it's definitely organisms; he has a low sperm count.'

Ashley realises he has been the victim of a wind-up, or has he?

Brian continues, 'Over breakfast Maggie said on her birthday in November she'll be eighteen. She has two elder sisters who're both married. She lives on the outskirts of that place north of Diss and works in Woolworths as a shop assistant.

Although we'd only just met I felt as if we'd been friends for a lot longer, she was so sweet and kind. After breakfast we went for a walk round the shopping centre and Saturday market. Maggie asked me if I had a girlfriend, I told her I did, but if she will be my girlfriend I'd do the decent thing and break up with her when I got home. I wanted to be truthful to both Maggie and Sylvia, the girl back home. I think this made a good impression on her.

As it happens Sylvia wasn't that bothered, as she was sweet on one of my old pals Johnny Orris. When we married Maggie moved in with me and my parents. Maggie always felt guilty about splitting us up, but she and Sylvia became very good friends. In the early seventies she more than made it up to her friend.

I asked her if she'd like to see me play darts in the afternoon, I was made up when she agreed. She told me her group of girl friends were going home by train tomorrow lunch time.

Suffolk's Last Cold War Victim

At 15:00 pm we arrived at the darts venue. I wasn't bothered about playing darts I just wanted to be alone with this wonderful gal. I was the third player to step up to the oche; the first two games had gone to our opponents. My team were desperate for a win, but I wanted to win even more so I could impress my date.

I played the best darts of my life and won both games to win the match. All the way through I heard my teammates cheering me on, but the biggest cheers came from Maggie, who gave me another big kiss as I left the stage.

That evening we spent the night dancing, drinking and talking. When I walked her back home I began to feel sad, wondering if I'd ever see her again. To my great surprise and delight she asked me if we could see each other again.

When I said I would love to, she gave me another one of her special kisses and handed me a piece of paper with her name, address and telephone number on it. She said the number was for a public phone box, three doors down from her house. "When someone answers, tell them my name and address and they'll come and fetch me." That's what we had to do in them days. We didn't have mobile phones and most people couldn't afford phones in their houses.

To cut a long story short, over the next few months we met up regularly in Lowestoft. We chose Lowestoft, as trains from both our homes travelled there. I took a train from Wickham Market and Maggie took one from that place north of Diss.

Suffolk's Last Cold War Victim

Six months after we first met, the fateful day came to pass when she asked me to travel to that place north of Diss to meet her parents. She knew if I really loved her, I'd have to conquer my fears and go. 'I'd love to', I told her, with my fingers crossed behind my back.

So two weeks later, I made the historic, or should I say 'horrific' journey to her home city. When I got off the train I saw Maggie waving to me from behind the barriers. 'Hello darling, so happy to see you. There's a bus leaving from the front of the station in five minutes, it stops close to my house. My parents are looking forward to meeting you.

We boarded the bus for the fifteen-minute journey to her house; I was quite surprised to see everyone acting normally. When we stepped off the bus, I saw a small playground on the opposite side of the road.

I heard the sound of an approaching helicopter flying fairly low overhead. Maggie told me this is normal as the airport is only a couple of miles away. What I saw next was unusual, the sight of two women dashing out of their houses and running onto the playground. They began throwing pieces of bread onto the ground; I believe they thought it was a large bird. Perhaps my original understanding of this tribe had been right all along.

We walked along a few streets before arriving at Maggie's, semi-detached council house. It had a fairly large front garden with a well-manicured lawn, bordered by lovely, scented flowerbeds.

Suffolk's Last Cold War Victim

When we went inside I was greeted by her parents, Ivan and Irene. Maggie was the spitting image of her mother. They were both very polite and I instantly felt comfortable in their presence. That evening we spent the evening in the local Labour working men's club.

We arrived in time to play a game of bingo. I was well chuffed when the last number to fill my card was called. "House" I shouted out loudly. I won ten shillings and sixpence. The locals weren't best pleased; they knew I was an intruder. I could feel the daggers in my back as I went up to collect my winnings. Unbeknown to me my blue and white Ipswich Town football scarf began unfurling from my coat pocket.

Following the bingo we were entertained by a Country and Western band, who were actually very good. We left the club about an hour before closing time, leaving her parents behind. As we walked back in the light of a full moon, a motor bike roared by. I was half expecting to see a yokel chasing it down the road.

When we arrived home, we had time for a kiss and cuddle before hearing Ivan, deliberately making a lot of noise with his keys whilst opening the front door.

I didn't sleep very well that night. It wasn't the strange bed I was laying in; it was the noise of some locals howling at the full moon.

You asked me earlier why and how I learned to speak posh, well I'll tell you. I knew my Suffolk dialect could get me in a few scrapes if I continued to do my courting in that place north of Diss. Maggie was a member of a local amateur

Suffolk's Last Cold War Victim

dramatics group; she asked them if I could join in. They said yes with one proviso, I had to take elocution lessons to lose my Suffolk brogue. It took many weeks, but finally I was accepted by everyone in the group. So there, that's how it happened.'

Before they knew it they had arrived in Belford. He asks Brian if he wants dropping off at his house. Brian replies, 'Yoo ken drop mee heeya if yer loike,' pointing to a spot just before a bus stop. 'Oy'll goo'n hev a mardle with Maggie.'

Ashley stops the car just before the bus stop and some villagers waiting for the bus. He releases Brian's seat belt before reaching over to open the door to let him out. Before closing the door Ashley calls out Brian, 'Thanks for your help today and I look forward to seeing you soon. Cheerio tergither.'

He has to wait for traffic to pass before he can drive off. As he waits he cannot help but notice the quizzical looks on their faces. It was if they had not seen Brian and thought he had been talking to himself.

Suffolk's Last Cold War Victim

Chapter 13

More villagers' secrets

When Ashley gets home he runs to the toilet, before unloading his shopping. He mutters to himself 'I hope when I get to Brian's age I'll have his constitution. Come to think of it, since arriving in the village I haven't seen him eat, drink or use the toilet.' His investigative mind begins asking all kinds of 'What if'-questions, but nothing made any sense. He decides to keep an eye on him in the future.

He grabs his tools and goes outside to install the new mailbox, fixing it to a thick wooden gate post. When he goes back inside, he notices he has a missed call and a voice mail message on his home phone.

The call and message is from Mark Haines. He presses play to listen to the message. 'Hello Ashley, only me. Just to let you know I'm running an article in this Sunday's edition, reminding people the gang are still at large and a reward for information leading to their capture is still available. I hope you're OK and I'm looking forward to seeing you soon. Keep safe, Mark.'

After his evening meal, he settles down to watch television and write his recollections of this morning's trip to Ipswich. As he writes he keeps laughing to himself as he recalls Brian's stories. He is pleased he has managed to complete ten pages of notes tonight, considerably more than previous attempts in the last few evenings.

The next morning, his alarm clock wakes him. This is a welcome change from the earlier wakeup calls by a Postman activated alarm. He cannot wait to see if there are any letters in his newly acquired mailbox.

After breakfast he sets off to the shops. As he closes the gates he opens his new mailbox, inside are two letters. He's pleased to see them, even though they are only invoices from a removals company and an aerial installer.

He takes a route that passes by Brian's house. He still has some concerns regarding his observations over the last few days. Standing outside his house he notices all the curtains are open, could this mean he's home? He walks down the garden path and rings the doorbell. A minute later, having had no response he uses the knocker.

As he waits for an answer he hears a women's voice calling out, 'Ashley, Brian's not there. He's gone to visit an old school friend in Bury St Edmunds. He's been gone a couple of weeks now, we don't know when he's coming back.' It was Nicola Scott. Ashley replies, 'Thanks Nicola, I just wanted to see if he was back.'

She continues, 'We all thought it strange when he went off, without cancelling his paper and milk deliveries. Geoffrey told us Brian informed his son, Peter that he was going away for a few weeks to stay with an old friend. It was Peter who did the decent thing and cancelled the deliveries for him.'

Suffolk's Last Cold War Victim

Ashley thanks Nicola for the information and hopes to see her again soon. As he continues walking to the shops he mutters, 'Nothing makes any sense. Why was Peter the only person he told he was going away? If he's not been home, where has he been staying and why am I the only person to have seen and spoken to him?'

He enters Mrs Sarah Noble Art gallery/ Bookshop. He briefly met Sarah Noble earlier in the week when he ordered Charlie Haylock's book, 'SLOIGHTLY ON TH'HUH', the one Brian recommended.

Sarah is busy dealing with another customer so he looks around the shop. He sees some lovely oil and watercolour paintings. There are also a number of sketches of the village's church and buildings. He was quite taken with the sketch of St. Mary's church with a price tag of £50. The artist's signature, Allen Harris is in the bottom left-hand corner. He continues looking and sees a watercolour painting with the same surname, his first name was Tony.

Mrs Noble greets Ashley and places his book on the counter. She asks, 'How are you settling in Mr Moore?' He replies, 'Very well, thank you for asking Mrs Noble.' She said, 'Oh please call me Sarah and I'll call you Ashley, if that's OK with you.' He says, 'I'm fine with that. I'd also like to purchase the St. Mary sketch.' After wrapping the sketch, she places it and the book in a large bag.

He said, 'I'm looking forward to reading my book tonight, I'm trying to become Suffolkated. My friend Brian Damant recommended it to me earlier this week.' She seemed

Suffolk's Last Cold War Victim

a bit surprised by this statement and asks, 'Oh Brian's back then? He usually pops in to say hello when he goes for his daily lunchtime pint in the pub. Perhaps he'll be in there tonight. It's karaoke on Saturdays and he does an excellent Elvis impersonation. You're quite welcome to join us. I'll introduce you to some of the locals if you like.' Ashley does not need to think about it and replies, 'I'd like that very much. What time does it start?' Sarah said, 'We normally arrive around 19:30 pm, I'll reserve a seat for you.'

Leaving the shop he has another 'What if?' to add to the ever growing list. 'Why has Brian not been going to the pub for his daily pint of Ghost Ship?'

All the talk of the pub and beer makes Ashley very thirsty, so he decides to pop in and have a quick half before heading home.

As he makes his way to the bar he notices there are only a handful of patrons in the pub. 'Micro' asks, 'Usual Ashley?' Ashley replies, 'Could you make it a half please, Bill? I'll be in later this evening for full measures.' He starts going red in the face when he realises what he just said. He hopes Bill has not taken it the wrong way, but he still watches him closely making sure the beer reaches the mark at the top of the glass.

Ashley asks Bill if Brian has been in for a drink recently. Bill did not have to think too long about this question as he replies, 'He hasn't been in here since Tuesday March 27th. He told me he was on the way to the Co-op, to buy his Euro lottery ticket. When he didn't come in the next day, I assumed

Suffolk's Last Cold War Victim

the old bugger had won the jackpot. It's been a few weeks now and I'm actually starting to believe it myself.'

He pays for his beer and sits on the sofa to enjoy his drink and read his new book. He finds the book very amusing as well as informative. After a few minutes he heard a familiar voice say, 'Oy towd yoo yoo'd loike ut.'

Ashley answers, 'Hello Brian, yes, it's very good. Would you like a drink?' 'Oi'm foine thank yer koindly...Oy saw yer an' thought Oy'd come in furra mardle.' Ashley says, 'I called round your house today, only to be told you'd gone to stay with an old friend in Bury St Edmunds.'

Brian responds, 'Wot a load o' ol' squit...Oy've bin jor'n with yoo awl week...So Oy caarn't o' bin in two playces at once...cood Oy?' Ashley could not argue with this logic, so moves on to another thing that's been worrying him. 'I was wondering why you haven't been seen by anyone around the village and Micro said he hadn't seen you since late March for your daily pint?'

'Oy caan't drink cause o' moy tablets o' tayke...fer this ere artheroytus... an' Oy doon't feel loike mix'n at present.'

This sort of made sense to Ashley and decides not to push him any further on the subject. Brian asks 'Ha'yer sin any new uns laytely?'

'Yes, I have actually. I've been introduced to Mrs Nicola Scott, Perry Lakeman, Adie Dale, Sarah Noble and Laura Archibald. I'd appreciate any snippets of information on their

Suffolk's Last Cold War Victim

characters. And please would you mind using your posh accent?'

The pub is starting to get busier. Ashley wonders why people are avoiding sitting too close to him and Brian. Then he overhears a woman whispering to her friend, 'Is he talking to himself?' Ashley glances over to the women, they quickly turn around to avoid eye contact with him.

Brian continues, 'Nicola is the most honest, trustworthy person you could ever meet. She's worked hard to represent this village and the people in it. She and her husband Colin live a few doors down from me. They've got twin daughters, who are both at university. They take after their mother which is just as well, as her husband's a sly, conniving, money grabbing cheat.

He's been receiving backhanders from businessmen and private householders. He wangles information from her on planning applications and lobbies his wife to get applications approved.

At 19:15 pm tonight he has a meeting on that table in the corner, the one next to the ladies' toilet, with a Property Developer. He'll be given an envelope full of cash. If only you were a newspaper journalist, you'd know how to get a good scoop.'

'Sorry to butt in Brian, but how do you know all this?'

'We posties know where to look when we're on our rounds and old habits die hard. A lot of people leave their curtains open with the lights on, if you're snouty like me you'll

Suffolk's Last Cold War Victim

see some things that'll make a bishop blush. When I'm sitting in a pub, I keep my ears and eyes open. That's how I know what's occurring. They'll be there tonight, at 19:15 pm on the dot.

If you had a hidden camera, you'd see I was right all along. It's about time someone takes him down a peg or two; it isn't as if he's short of money. I think he does it because he's jealous of his wife's popularity and political career.'

Ashley thinks this is too good an opportunity for him to miss out on. He decides to record the meeting. He did not know what he'll do with the information if Brian's accusations are proved to be correct. Right or wrong one thing he knows for sure, he could use a flawed character in his novel.

Ashley shows Brian the sketch he bought in Sarah's shop. Brian tells him, 'That was drawn by a local artist he's one of three brothers, all artists who live in the village.

Allen, the eldest does sketches; the middle Brother Tony uses watercolours.' He begins talking about another subject before Ashley asks 'Excuse me Brian; I thought I heard you say there're three brothers. Who's the third and what sort of artist is he?'

As he begins answering, he sees Brian's shoulders begin shrugging up and down, 'Ah yes the third and youngest brother, his name's Adrian, AKA FOK he's a 'Piss artist'.' he lifts an imaginary glass as if he's drinking from it. Ashley let out a large laugh, loud enough to make some patrons turn round to see who is laughing.

Suffolk's Last Cold War Victim

When he finishes giggling, he said, 'I know I'm going to regret asking this, but why is he also known as FOK?'

Brian replies, 'Adrian's very smart he knows everything, FOK stands for 'Fountain of Knowledge'. At our regular pub quizzes he's barred from entering, making it fairer for everyone else, so he has to sit at the bar. When the answers are checked if a question hasn't been answered by any team, the quizmaster reads out the question again and asks, does anyone know the answer? everyone points at him and shouts out, "FOK knows."

Brian continues, 'You said you met Perry Lakeman our old landlord. He's the sort of man you want with you if you're in trouble. A gentle giant until provoked. You didn't have to worry about being given short measures, unlike 'Micro' over there.

Perry would let you have drinks on the slate and stand you a drink if you were short of a bob or two. We all enjoyed the lock-ins at the weekends. He never had any trouble with the police; in fact the local bobby would often join us when he'd finished his shift.

Adie Dale was a second-hand car salesman. In 1972, following the deaths of his parents in a fire at their home in Woodbridge, he came to the village to live with his Auntie, Jo Middleton.

Jo was the step-sister of Adie's dad Gordon. She was a spinster and glad of the company of a seventeen-year-old. They quickly developed a loving bond.

Suffolk's Last Cold War Victim

Having completed a car mechanic apprenticeship at Ipswich College, he began working for a well-known Ford dealership in Woodbridge. Shortly after finishing his apprenticeship he realised working in a workshop wasn't for him. He wanted to work in the sales department, believing it to be more glamorous. Here he wouldn't have to spend hours covered in oil and grease instead; he'd be dressed in smart suits and put his natural gift of the gab to full use.

And boy, he certainly knew how to use his patter to sell new and used cars for the dealership. He also used it to seduce the girls. He'd bring a different girl to the pub every other week. It seems he was unable or unwilling to commit to a long-term relationship.

He decided he could make more money if he bought and sold his own cars. So he handed in his notice and went out on his own. We weren't sure if John Sullivan the writer of Only Fools and Horses moulded the character of "Boycie" on Adie, or was Adie the one copying his hero Boycie?

Over the years he became so successful selling cars he was able to retire at the age of fifty. This was just as well, as he was able to care for Auntie Jo, whose health began to deteriorate, unfortunately she died four years ago.

Adie got bored doing nothing, so he applied and got a job investigating 'Cock-ups.' Ashley interrupts, 'Did he work for an insurance company investigating accidents?' Brian replies, 'No, he got a job designing condoms for a well-known company.' Ashley wonders if this is true or has he once again been a victim of another Brian wind-up.

Suffolk's Last Cold War Victim

Brian continues. 'He's been doing a lot of testing lately, with the help of Micro's missus. Poor old Bill hasn't been able to perform his bedroom duties since his accident. Betty's happy with the attention shown to her, but to him, she's just another notch on his bed post.'

Knowing he would be returning later that evening, Ashley informs Brian he's going home for some dinner, and would he like to come back and join him. As expected, Brian declines his offer.

Finishing his drink he puts his new book back in the bag, and turns to his friend and says, 'Cheerio Brian. See you again soon.' But he is nowhere to be seen. A lot more people are beginning to look at him with quizzical looks on their faces.

On the way out, he looks for places to conceal his recording device during this evening's dodgy deal. Between the ladies' toilet door and the table where Brian has indicated the meeting will take place, there is a row of coat hangers. He decides this would be an ideal place to hang his coat with the recording device inside it.

Suffolk's Last Cold War Victim

Chapter 14

New friends – hidden talents

On the way home he tries to work out how Brian gets in and out of his home without being detected. And how does he manage to disappear as quickly as he did just then in the pub? On a lighter note he keeps grinning to himself as he recalls Brian anecdotes.

When he arrived home he searches high and low for his recording device. He finally finds it in a box in the garage. He never expected he'd be using it so quickly, or indeed ever again.

Because it has taken him so long to find it there is no time to prepare a meal. He's not that bothered as he can have a meal later in the pub.

He enters the pub at 19:00 pm and spots Colin Scott seating at the exact table Brian said he would. Better still he was sat with his back to the coat hangers, giving an uninterrupted view for his camera to record the meeting.

Ashley walks over and hangs his coat on a coat peg, carefully positioning it to face the table. He switches the device to record and then walks to the bar to order a drink.

He is surprised to be served by Bill's wife Betty. He desperately wants to ask how the condom testing is going, but just said, 'Hello Mrs Gates, my name's Ashley, I've recently

Suffolk's Last Cold War Victim

arrived in the village. Although I've been in here several times, this is the first time we've met. Can I have a pint of Ghost Ship and take one for you and I'd like a prawn salad please?'

Mrs Gates replies, 'That's very kind of you Ashley. Please call me Betty. How are you settling in?'

He answers, 'Amazingly well, everyone's been very welcoming. In fact, I've been invited to join Sarah Noble and her friends this evening.'

'Well, you haven't got long to wait, she's just walked in. There's your beer, that's twelve pounds and twenty pence please,' said Betty.

Looking towards the door, he sees Sarah walking towards him. Following closely behind is a gentleman in a light grey suit. His first thoughts were, 'Are they together?' but the man keeps walking past when Sarah reaches the bar.

The man goes to the far end of the bar and orders two pints of beer, before sitting down next to Colin. Checking his watch Ashley is gobsmacked to see it is 19:15 pm exactly. 'How did he know?' thought Ashley

Turning his attention to his guest he says, 'Hello Sarah, thanks once again for inviting me tonight. Can I get you a drink?' She replies, 'That's kind of you, but we normally wait until everyone's here, then we all put fifteen pounds in the kitty for the drinks. At the end of the evening if there's any money left over, it goes in a collection box. The village has just started a collection for a Youth clubhouse. We need forty-five

Suffolk's Last Cold War Victim

thousand pounds to purchase a purpose built Portacabin, to be located on the left-hand side of the village green.'

'That sounds good, I've got time to eat my meal and finish this one.' Turning his attention back to the two men, he is surprised the man in the suit has drunk his beer and is about to walk out of the door, followed closely by Colin Scott.

Ashley walked over to his coat and pretends to get something out of his pockets. In fact, he is merely switching the device off. He hopes it has successfully recorded their meeting and he cannot wait to get home to review it.

Over the next ten minutes five more people arrive to join Sarah's group. The first to arrive is Sarah's daughter, Kathryn (Kat) French and her husband Glenn. Then David Gale and his wife Rebecca arrive and finally a familiar face he is very pleased to see, Laura Archibald.

Sarah says, 'Welcome everyone. Tonight I'm pleased to introduce you to Ashley, who moved to the village on Monday. Ashley, would you like to tell the group a few things about yourself? You don't need to stand up, unless you want to.'

He is more than happy to remain seated. He begins, 'Hello everyone, as Sarah said, my name's Ashley and I've just moved to Old Oak Lane. I recently retired from the Civil Service and that's all I can say on this subject. Since I arrived here I've been made to feel very welcome by everyone. Under the guidance of an elderly villager, I'm hoping to be Suffolkated. I love my new home, the people and the village, but most of all, I love Ghost Ship. When your introductions are

Suffolk's Last Cold War Victim

over please let me treat you all to a drink, before we use the money in the kitty.'

David Gale said, 'Hello Ashley, my name's David Gale and this is my lovely wife, Rebecca. I'm the headmaster of Heathlands High School in Wickham Market.'

The next introduction is by Rebecca. 'Welcome Ashley. My name's Rebecca and I am a senior nurse at Ipswich's Heath Road hospital. We have an eighteen-year-old son Melvin, who is about to go to Northampton University.'

Looking over to the person next to Rebecca, Sarah's daughter raises her hand and says, 'Hello, my name's Kathryn French, my friend's call me Kat. I work in a care home for the elderly specialising in Alzheimer's and Dementia. This is my husband Glenn, over to you darling.'

'Hi Ashley as Kat said, my name's Glenn, I'm a Train Conductor for Greater Anglia based at Ipswich station. One day I hope to train to be a driver. We're currently living with my mother-in-law Sarah while we save for a deposit to buy our own home. I'll now hand you over to this wonderful lady...'

Before he can mention her name Ashley said, 'Yes, I've already met this wonderful talented lady, hello again Laura.' He smiles at her. 'Hello again Ashley, I thought our date was tomorrow,' she said, returning his smile, making him blush once more and causes the others to look inquisitively at each other.

Suffolk's Last Cold War Victim

With the introductions over, Ashley asks everyone what they would like to drink. Sarah hands him a sheet of paper with everyone's preference. 'Please add your choice to the list,' she said.

'I'll give you a hand,' Laura offers. Ashley welcomes her offer of help and they set off to the bar. He is surprised with Laura's choice of drink, half a pint of 'Ghost Ship.' She said, 'I think I take after my dad. Hold on, that's not right, I've just realised, he only drank lager.'

The evening was really enjoyable and relaxing, Ashley even has a go at Karaoke. He sang David Bowie's "Life on Mars" with the help of three pints of 'Ghost Ship'. At the end of the evening the Youth clubhouse fund has increased by fifteen pounds and sixty pence from the unspent kitty. Ashley does the gentlemanly thing and walks Laura home, even though it is just around the corner.

When he arrives home he is still on a high. He is desperate to listen to the surveillance recording, but decides to leave it until tomorrow. Instead, he opens his notebook and enters twelve more characters for his novel. He then goes to bed to continue reading his new book.

Suffolk's Last Cold War Victim

Chapter 15

Births deaths and marriages

Early Sunday morning Ashley's alarm rings at the usual time of 07:30 am, he turns it off and goes back to sleep. When he eventually wakes, the clock is showing 09:45 am. He temporary forgets which day it is, then the penny drops, it's Sunday. He told Laura he would be attending the morning service.

He quickly showers and gets dressed. He has a couple of rounds of toast before heading off to the church service. Outside the weather is very windy with dark grey clouds. To be on the safe side he takes an umbrella with him, just in case it rains.

He arrives just in time to introduce himself to the verger, Mr Eric Osben. Laura is already sitting at the organ playing some music, so did not see him enter and take a seat behind her.

St. Mary's vicar, Michael Moss, welcomes the twenty-six members of the congregation. The service lasts just over an hour. During the last hymn he sings the words very loudly, hoping Laura will recognise his voice. It works she turns round smiles at him and mouths, 'Hello.'

Ashley makes sure he is the last of the congregation to leave the service. He wants to introduce himself to the vicar

Suffolk's Last Cold War Victim

and thank him for an uplifting service today. The vicar is pleased to meet him and for the feedback on his service.

Laura is the last to leave, she sees Ashley waiting for her. 'Hello Ashley, I was beginning to think you'd stood me up,' she said, laughing loudly. 'Sorry about that, but it was so comfortable and snug in bed I decided to have a lay in. It's starting to rain; would you like to share my umbrella?' he asks.

Quick as a flash she joins him under his umbrella. Now she is close to him her perfume fills his nostrils, bringing back memories of his beloved Susan.

'Do you have any plans for the rest of the day?' he asks. She replies, 'I've been invited to Kat and Glenn's for dinner, then this evening I've a lot of marking to finish and preparing lessons for the coming week. Would you like to meet up one night this week? Perhaps you'd like me to cook you a meal'

'I'd like that very much' he said. When they reach her front gate she asks him to exchange phone numbers. She said she will ring to confirm a day that's suitable for both of them.

On the way home he goes into the Co-op to buy a copy of The World of News. He flips through the pages until he finds the story of the gang's escape and the reward on offer for their arrest, just as Mark had promised.

Arriving home he goes into the kitchen to make a cup of tea and a bacon sandwich. As he looks out of the kitchen window, he catches sight of a figure walking past. He jumps

Suffolk's Last Cold War Victim

back as this has really spooked. Then he sees the figure is none other than his friend Brian.

He opens the back door to let him in. 'Brian, what are you doing out in this weather with just a light jacket on? Come in, you must be freezing. Would you like a cup of tea?' Brian replies, 'Oy'm okay thankyer koindly....Yoo're roight...thas frawn out theya...Oy wanted to see heow yer got on yessdee.'

Seeing Brian reminds Ashley he wants to ask him about a comment he made on Friday. 'Brian before we listen to the tapes, I'm curious about something you said on the way back from Ipswich. It's regarding Maggie and what she did for Sylvia in the seventies? Can you please use your posh voice again, as it makes it easier for me to write it down?'

'Well, I'll tell you, as I need to finally get it off my chest. For many years Maggie and Sylvia tried but were unable to conceive and have children. In Maggie's case her fallopian tubes were defective Her doctor told her condition was incurable. We talked about adoption, but she didn't want to go down that route. I think she was hoping for a miracle but as the years went by, she went off the whole idea of having children.

Sylvia on the other hand was OK; it was Johnny who was firing blanks. In July 1972 the two women began talking to each other about their shared problems. One day, Maggie suggested to Sylvia she could solve their problem, by getting me to become a sperm donor.

Suffolk's Last Cold War Victim

The next day, Sylvia and Johnny called round to give Maggie their answer. It was a resounding yes. Maggie was relieved; all they needed to do now was get me to agree.

When I got home from work, they were waiting for me. As I listened to each of them giving me their reasons for this strange request, all I kept thinking was it's a long time since I got my leg over with another women and my wife is organising it for me.

The women worked out the day she'd be most fertile. When that day arrived, I had a bath and changed my pants before we went round. I was so excited walking up the front path.

Maggie asked if Sylvia and Johnny were both ready? They nodded and went into the bedroom. I thought this isn't right, I can't perform with all of them watching me.

They never once suggested artificial insemination, until Maggie said, 'Right Brian, you come with me.' With that she took me into another bedroom. She laid me on the bed, took my trousers and pants off and began to fondle my crown jewels with one hand, whilst unscrewing the cap off a small glass jar with the other.

"Tell me when you're near they need all you've got". That's when the penny dropped. I felt deflated, almost literally. It was only when Maggie said, "Don't worry, we'll do it properly when we get home", that I managed to finish the deed.

Suffolk's Last Cold War Victim

She put the cap back on the jar and gave it to Johnny in the other bedroom. She wished them good luck and we left them to it.

On the way home I asked, 'What's going to happen now?' She said, 'Sylvia's bought a basting tube and as we speak, Johnny is filling it with your sperm. Then he will insert it you know where and empty it.'

The operation was successful and that's how Maggie finally got rid of her guilt. Nobody in the village had any suspicions of this unusual conception. The happy parents remained our best friends until their deaths a few years ago. You're the only person I have ever told this story to.'

'Wow' said Ashley. 'That's an amazing story; you and Maggie are both incredible people. Wow.' He mutters again.

Ashley went into the living room to fetch the surveillance device. He takes the Sim card out and inserts it into his laptop. 'Right, let's listen to these recordings. I hope we've something audible. Ashley is pleased when the recording shows Colin's left hand side profile. The lighting is also very good; he hopes the audio is as good. At first he can only make out the muffled background noise of people talking in the distance.

Then he sees another man join him at the table. The audio level is clear enough for them to follow their conversation.

Colin

Suffolk's Last Cold War Victim

Hello Steve, you're looking well. I've got some information for you. I think you'll be pleased with it.

Steve
I hope so; I've been waiting a long time to get this project approved. So, what have you got for me?

Colin
Since we last spoke, I've been working on the old girl to get her to re-examine your application. I told her if she and the rest of the planning committee didn't pull their fingers out and start building some new social housing, the government will bypass them and build who knows where. I told her if her committee agrees to use your land, they wouldn't have the government sniffing around everything her committee's been working on. So, on Thursday having consulted with some of her trusted friends, she got her committee to agree and they passed a resolution to approve your proposal. You should have it in the next two weeks.

Steve
Well done, Colin, I knew I could rely on you. Here's the first payment. Five grand now, twenty grand when I get the final go ahead. Nice doing business with you. I might ask for your help again in a few months, if you're interested.

    Ashley and Brian watch as Steve passes an envelope to Colin. He looks around to see if anyone is watching, before he fingers the money inside, then places the envelope in an inside pocket of his jacket.

Suffolk's Last Cold War Victim

Brian said, 'He keeps all his ill-gotten gains in a safe built into a large desk in the front room of his home; he's got over fifty thousand pounds in it. Nicola doesn't know anything about the safe or what's inside it.'

Ashley asks, 'Brian, do you know who this Steve is?' 'I do. He's name is Steven Rogers, a Property Developer. He's a nasty piece of work; a few years ago, he pressured an elderly, widowed lady into selling a large piece of her land for a lot less than its true value.

This isn't the first time he's done this sort of thing; I've got names, places and the amount of money involved. If I were a newspaper owner, I'd expose him for what he really is.'

Ashley is thrown by this last statement. He wants to ask him, 'Do you know what I used to do and that I've a close friend who's a newspaper editor? How did you get the information on Rogers, and is it all true?'

He wonders how he can get this information to Mark Haines without dropping Nicola Scott in it. Then he suddenly remembers he's not in this game anymore.

Ashley said, 'It's getting on. Would you like me to continue with the other people I met, or would you prefer to come round another time?'

Brian answers, 'I'd prefer to keep going, as I don't know how much longer I've got.'

Ashley is in a quandary. Is Brian referring to the time left today, or is his arthritis more serious than he is letting on?

Suffolk's Last Cold War Victim

Ashley informs him, 'Before I start I'm just going to put the Sim card back in the recorder and tape this session. Ok, these are the villagers I met last night. The person who invited me to join them, Sarah Noble, the book shop owner, her daughter and son-in-law, Kathryn and Glenn French, David and Rebecca Gale and finally, Laura Archibald.'

Brian says, 'Let's start with Laura. Philip and Laura met when his father, an American pilot, transferred to Bentwaters air base. The family moved to the village, renting a house close to Laura's home.

Philip was just one of a few black pupils at her school; he was very shy and a little bit frightened, until Laura made friends with him.

They were in the same class at school, sitting next to each other for most lessons. He wasn't as clever as her, so she helped him with his homework after school. She never gave him the answers only giving him explanations, until he understood the subject better.

As the months went by his confidence grew, and he was less dependent on Laura's help. In 1990 they both achieved the grades needed to qualify for a university place.

The timing couldn't have been better, as his father was about to be posted to Germany. Instead of going with the family Philip asked his father, if he could stay and go to university in England, his father gave him his blessing. He gained a place at Newham University, in Birmingham to study for an engineering degree. He chose this university so he could

Suffolk's Last Cold War Victim

be with his girlfriend Laura, who was studying for her teaching degree.

Three years later, they both obtained their degrees. Following a gap year travelling round New Zealand, they looked forward to returning home. On the last day of the trip, Philip proposed to Laura and she accepted. He couldn't bear to be apart from her and once they were married, he applied for Dual citizenship. When they returned home they both found employment in Suffolk.

After their wedding they lived with her parents, whilst saving for a house of their own. In 1996 they'd saved enough money for a deposit on a two-bed roomed house in the village.'

Brian gave a long sigh before continuing. 'There's a sad tale behind each of these lovely people. Have you heard anything about the tragic loss of Sarah and Laura's husbands?

'No, I haven't, although I knew her husband was dead she never told me any details surrounding his death.'

'Well, it all happened one Sunday morning in October 2014. Sarah's husband Darren, her son-in-law Glenn and Laura's husband Philip were fishing in a small boat, about a mile off Felixstowe beach. They'd been fishing for about two hours when all of a sudden, a violent squall rolled in. As the sea began to get very choppy the men decided to make a run for the shore.

When they hauled up the anchor, things took a turn for the worse. The waves were getting really rough, with white

Suffolk's Last Cold War Victim

horses breaking all around. To make matters worse their outboard motor wouldn't start, so Darren began to row.

Then they were hit broadside on by a large wave. All three were thrown into the sea before they had a chance to send out a distress signal.

A person on the shore was watching the unfolding disaster and dialled 999 to report it to the coastguards. A lifeboat was sent out from the Harwich RNLI Station.

Unfortunately, by the time the lifeboat arrived on the scene, the only person they could save was Glenn. Darren had a cardiac arrest in the water and was pronounced dead when they pulled him onto the lifeboat. Philip's lifeless body was found by the lifeboat crew an hour after the capsizing. He'd received a massive head wound. At the inquest the Coroner concluded, his injuries had been caused by the anchor striking him as the boat turned over.

Glenn still suffers from survivor's guilt. That's why he looks after both the widows' needs. He does all their gardening, DIY and taxiing requirements.

A few years prior Laura lost both parents within a short time then this tragedy happened. The only thing keeping her sane is her faith and the support of her church friends. My only hope is, she finds a like-minded person to make her happy again.

David's a lovely gentleman who's devoted to his profession and students, past and present. His wife Rebecca, a nurse is also a dedicated professional.

Suffolk's Last Cold War Victim

They have a son, Melvin, who is about to suffer the biggest misfortune of his life, that'll have an enormous impact on both his parents.' 'What's he going to do?' asks Ashley.

'Next Friday week there's a going away party, for the local villagers who're about to start university. When I was in Wickham Market last week, I overheard two lads talking about spiking Melvin's drink, in revenge for Melvin taking his girlfriend away from him and for being the son of their former headmaster.

As he doesn't drink, he'll be driving his car to the party with two girl passengers from the village. If he drives home under the influence of the drugs, there's a good chance he could kill or seriously injure himself or someone else.

Melvin could face a term in prison and the humiliation will cause his father to resign from his job. He's a bright, intelligent lad, who's always been helpful and polite. If someone can stop him from attending the party, or stop the lads giving him the drugs, he and his parents can continue to be pillars of the community.'

'Where and when is this party taking place?' he asks. 'Friday 4th May at the Bandbox nightclub in Woodbridge,' replies Brian.

Ashley pauses for a few moments before answering, 'I'll see what I can do,' he remembers Craig Ferguson will be calling round next Sunday.

Brian said, 'George...yoo're look'n as if yoo're goo'n ter drowp orf...Oy'll leave yer to ut...Praps Oy'll see yer Toosdee.'

Suffolk's Last Cold War Victim

Ashley agrees and asks if he can show him round some of the local attractions. Brian replies, 'We'll start in Orford, if that's OK with you. Right, that's me done, cheerio tergither.'

With that, Ashley opens the front door to let his friend out and presses the remote to open the gates. Watching him walk down the path, he wonders if Brian will still be wearing the same clothes he has been wearing all week.

Looking at his to do list, he remembers he has to call Mark to thank him for printing the story today.

The phone rang three times before Mark answers. Ashley says 'Hi Mark just a quick call to thank you for running the story today. I was wondering if you'd be available to come and visit me this Sunday, Laptop's coming too. There's something I need to run past you both.'

Mark says, 'That sounds intriguing. I hope everything is all OK with you?'

'Yes, every thing's fine here. It's just I've acquired some information that may prove useful to you both, but I need some advice on how to proceed with it. You won't be disappointed.'

'OK Ashley, as my work on the paper's done on Saturday, I'll come, but only if you buy me lunch, a few pints of Ghost Ship and a bed for the night.'

'Great, I look forward to seeing you then. Laptop's arriving around midday. Why don't you give him a call, perhaps you can come together in one car.'

Suffolk's Last Cold War Victim

'That's a good idea, Ashley; I'll give him a call right now. Look after yourself mate; I'll see you see soon.'

He is feeling really hungry, then he remembers he has not had anything to eat or drink for ages. As it's nearly 19:00 pm, it' a no brainer, go to the pub.

Suffolk's Last Cold War Victim

Chapter 16

The Orford merman

Monday morning is warm and sunny. Ashley has been listening to so many stories over the last week he's struggling to get his head round them all. They range from both ends of the tear producing spectrum, extremely sad to very funny.

After breakfast he decides to go for a long walk to recharge his batteries. He began by walking to the shops, passing Brian's house on the other side of the road. He sees Peter Hungerford's van parked outside, he's not in the front garden so assumes he's round the back.

As he crosses the road he spots Peter exiting Brian's front door, looking rather sheepish. He is almost within touching distance of Ashley who said, 'Morning Peter.' But Peter keeps his head down and completely ignores him, before getting in his van and driving off.

His old investigative alarm bells began ringing loudly. He knows if it does not look or feel right, you start asking questions. He makes a mental note to ask Brian about it tomorrow.

Stopping outside Sarah's shop, he enters and says, 'Hello Sarah. I just wanted to thank you for a thoroughly enjoyable evening on Saturday.' She replies, 'I'm glad you

Suffolk's Last Cold War Victim

enjoyed yourself and we look forward to seeing you again. What are you doing today?'

He says, 'As it's a lovely day, I thought I'd go for a nice long walk. By the way, can you tell me where the nearest Barber Shop is?'

'Well quite a few of the villagers use Andrea Godwell, she runs a mobile Hairdressing business for both men and women. I'll give you her number if you like.'

'That would be very helpful. I'll give her a call when I get home. Right, I'll leave you to it. See you later, bye.' With that he leaves the shop, popping the card with Andrea's number on it into his wallet.

After walking for ten minutes or so he reaches the outskirts of the village. He spots a signpost which read, 'Kelway 2½ Miles'. 'That's where I'll go then', he mutters to himself. The footpath starts in a small wood and continues across a wheat field.

The Suffolk countryside is generally flat, making the sky seem massive. Today as he looks up into a cloudless sky, all he can see are aircraft con trails crisscrossing the sky. In his mind it looks like look are playing a game of noughts and crosses.

After walking across the wheat field, he continues on a pathway through a meadow. In the middle of the meadow, he walks off the pathway for roughly thirty yards into the long grass. He lies down on his back looking up to the sky. The wildflowers are just tall enough to hide him from anybody walking by.

Suffolk's Last Cold War Victim

The silence is deafening, the fragrance from the flowers is quite exquisite. It is the perfect location for him to work out, how he's going to present the evidence of fraud to his friends next week, without implicating Nicola Scott.

Within a short time, he has worked out a strategy to implicate Steve Rogers in a number of fraud offences, and punish Colin Scott without involving his wife.

Feeling very satisfied that he has dealt with this subject his thoughts turn to Brian and Peter Hungerford.

- What was Peter doing in Brian's house today and why was he looking so shifty?
- Why did Brian tell him and no one else he was going away?
- What is the real story regarding Brian's health?
- Why do the villagers look at me as if I am talking to myself, whenever I'm with Brian?

The answer to these questions will take a lot more time and effort to work out.

He unlocks his mobile phone, opens the voice recorder app and begins dictating a letter to Colin Scott.

He is content knowing he has hopefully solved one of his problems. He continues on his journey to Kelway, reaching the village just after noon; he cannot believe how small the village is.

He counts twenty houses on the only road through the village. There are no shops, pubs, businesses or a church. 'I don't think I'll be coming here again', he mutters to himself.

Suffolk's Last Cold War Victim

It did however have a bus stop. He checks the timetable and as luck would have it, the second of three buses stopping here today, is due in ten minutes and it calls at Belford.

Finally arriving home at 14:00 pm, he unpacks his shopping and makes himself a cheese and onion crisp sandwich. When he finishes it, he dials the number Sarah gave him earlier for Andrea, the hairdresser.

When she answers Ashley said, 'Hello is this Andrea? 'Yes' came the reply. He continues, 'I've been given your number by Sarah Noble, a customer of yours from Belford. I've recently moved there and I'm hoping I can book an appointment with you to cut my hair.'

'Well, I'm in the village on Wednesday afternoon and I've had a cancellation for 14:30 pm. Will that work for you?'

'That'll be perfect thank you. My name is Ashley Moore. I live at 14 Old Oak Lane. I look forward to seeing you then, goodbye.'

He is pleased this has been sorted, as his hair is now longer than it has ever been in his whole life. Plus the dye is starting to grow out and requires some attention.

The walk and the rest in the meadow today, certainly had the desired effect in recharging his batteries. He opens his laptop and types the letter he dictated earlier.

He listens to the recordings of the meeting again to make sure he has not missed anything. He keeps the recording going so he can write down Brian's stories from yesterday.

Suffolk's Last Cold War Victim

He is really disappointed when he discovers Brian's voice did not record. He thought there may have been a fault with the recording device, until he heard his voice asking Brian some questions and other background noises on the playback.

He mutters, 'None of this makes any sense. Why is my voice on the recording but not Brian's? It isn't as though he's softly spoken. It's just another mystery to add to the ever-growing list.'

He makes a valiant effort to remember and record Brian's stories. Listening to the questions he'd asked Brian helps with his recollections.

At 20:30 pm the phone rings; it is Laura inviting him to join her on Wednesday evening for dinner. He said, 'I'd love to. Would you like me to bring red or white wine?' Laura said, 'I'd prefer a bottle of Ghost Ship, if you don't mind.' He replies, 'I don't mind in the least. That sounds great.'

When the call was over Ashley returns to his writing but finds it really hard to concentrate. All he can think about is his invitation to Laura's on Wednesday. Eventually he gives up and goes for a bath and an early night.

Tuesday's weather is similar to Monday he hopes it will stay this way for his sightseeing trip. Driving to pick up his travel companion, he is surprised to see Brian waiting by his front gate. He notices Brian's still wearing the same clothes again today.

Ashley opens the car door and welcomes Brian in, before securing his seat belt for him. As they set off Brian asks,

Suffolk's Last Cold War Victim

'Thas a noice day for ut George...Do yoo still wanna goo ter Orford?'

He replies, 'Yes please I'm really looking forward to it.' Then the Satnav announces, 'In one hundred yards turn left.' Brian jumps. 'Cood blaast mee...wot woz zat?'

Ashley explains, 'It's my Satnav, giving me directions to Orford and (pointing) this screen, shows me where we are on the scrolling map.' A mesmerised Brian replies, 'Cood blaast mee...wot'll they think o' next...a car that'll droive utself Oy s'pose.'

As they continue, Ashley can see Brian shaking his head every time the Satnav gave an instruction. He calms down and reverts to using his posh voice. Brian said, 'George, turn that old squit off. I'll give you the directions to Orford, but I'll take you on a more interesting route.' To keep the peace, Ashley agreed to his request. He's glad he did, as Brian had an interesting tale about every town and village they passed through.

Brian said 'This was my delivery area for many years. For most of the year it was a pleasure driving around the villages, delivering the post and speaking to the people. But when it snowed, it was hell. The wind would blow the snow off the fields, filling the little lanes and roads with deep snow drifts, often making them impassable.'

Ashley asks him if he missed the job when he retired. He replies, 'I didn't for the first two months, then I became a victim of Domestos abuse.'

Suffolk's Last Cold War Victim

Ashley said, 'Sorry Brian, don't you mean Domestic abuse.' Brian came back, 'No, it was definitely Domestos abuse. She made me do all the cleaning.' Ashley can see Brian shoulders shrugging again.

When they arrive at their destination in Orford, Ashley pulls into the Castle's car park. 'Wow, that's the loveliest little castle I've ever seen.' remarks Ashley. He asks Brian if he knows anything about its history. Brian says 'All I know is that it was built in the twelfth century by King Henry II. The only other thing I know, is the mystery of the 'Orford Merman'.

Don't look at me like that, it's a true story, if you don't believe me, buy a book in the shop over there,' pointing to the ticket office.

Ashley never knows when to believe him, even when he's being serious; such is the life of a wind-up merchant. He tells Brian he does believe him and looks forward to him telling the story as they walk round the castle.

He goes to the office and buys two entry tickets and a souvenir book. As he quickly flicks through the book, he sees the Merman on one of pages.

As they walk through the gates to the castle, the attendant calls out, 'Excuse me sir, you bought two tickets.' Ashley is surprised and answers, 'That's correct, one for me and one for my friend here', pointing to Brian.

The poor man is gobsmacked and just gives a thumbs up before turning away, shaking his head as he walks back to the office.

Suffolk's Last Cold War Victim

Ashley tries to imagine what the castle looked like when it was first built. He cannot wait to climb the five floors to see the views when they reach the top, and listen to Brian's Merman story.

It was worth the climb to the top to see the magnificent 360-degree views. He takes lots of photographs using his mobile phone and looks forward to reviewing them, when he gets home.

When he had got his breath back, Ashley said, 'OK Brian, tell me the Merman story.'

He began, 'In 1197 some local fishermen caught this naked, hairy man-like creature in their fishing nets. When they got back to shore they asked some soldiers, based in the castle for help.

They managed to constrain the beast, before locking it away in one the castle's cells. Over the next six months it was fed on raw fish and subjected to torture every day. The soldiers were trying to get it to speak, but it never did.

Then one day a soldier forgot to lock the cell door. The creature ran out of the door and headed straight for the sea; it entered the water and swam away, never to be seen again.

Some people reckon it was a bear or a type of monkey, that had escaped or fallen from a passing ship. If you ask me, I know exactly what it was.' He paused for a while, before Ashley, desperate to know said, 'What Brian, what do you think it was.'

Suffolk's Last Cold War Victim

'Well, all the signs are there; hairy, illiterate, not used to cooked food, it has to be someone from that place north of Diss.'

Ashley should have known better when he sees Brian's shoulders shrugging up and down. He'd been caught again, but still admires Brian's talent for keeping a straight face, whilst telling his stories.

As they make their way out of the exit, Ashley thanks the man in the office, telling him they had both enjoyed the tour of the castle. Once again the man just stares at him without saying a word. Ashley looking at Brian says, 'That's a bit rude.'

He asks Brian how he is doing for time. He said 'I'm OK, I've nothing planned for the rest of the day. I'll tell you what George let's go back via the old USAF Bentwaters airbase. Then we'll go to Eyke, I know there's an old nuclear shelter near there.'

Ashley remembers his father taking him to an air show at Bentwaters in the late seventies. 'Yes that would be great, thanks.'

It did not take long to reach the old airbase. Ashley can barely recognise the place, many of the buildings have been demolished or modernised for civilian use. The facility was demilitarised in 1993. The visit was a bit of an anti-climax. Maybe the nuclear shelter will be more interesting.

Before they leave the airbase, Brian points over to the east and asks if he can see Rendlesham forest in the distance,

Suffolk's Last Cold War Victim

Ashley said he can. Brian said, 'There was an incident in December 1980, when airmen from the base claimed to have witnessed sightings of a UFO.

Ashley did not say anything for a while; he is waiting for the punch line. He realises this may not be another windup and promises him he will research it when gets home.

When they reached the outskirts of Eyke, a village to the east of Bentwaters airbase, Brian asks him to pull over. Pointing up he said, 'Aircraft taking off or landing passed over this spot. I used to park my van here and watch the planes coming and going. I could feel the planes as they flew a few feet overhead, but it's a lot quieter these days.'

Continuing their journey, Brian directs him down a narrow lane with tall trees and thick vegetation along both sides. An old rusty sign hangs on a wire fence warning the public, 'MOD property. No Entry'.

After approximately 400 yards, Brian points left to an old five bar wooden gate that has been left open and tells him, 'Turn down there, until you can see two old telegraph poles on the right.

Right George, that'll do. Now can you see that old pillbox, under those bushes?' Ashley nods his head, to confirm he has seen it.

'Between the telegraph poles there's a small brick-built structure that looks like a cabinet with metal doors. If you didn't know, you'd think it housed telegraph wire connections. It didn't, behind the doors are a set of steps, leading to an

Suffolk's Last Cold War Victim

underground nuclear shelter. Do you think you could find this place again on your own?'

Ashley answered, 'Yes, I'm sure I could, but I don't know if I'd like to come here again. I'm getting pins and needles again and I've got a horrible feeling something really gruesome happened here.

OK Brian, I don't know about you, but I think we should start making our way home now.' Brian agrees, so they set off on the return journey to Belford. Ashley drops Brian off outside his house and watches him walking down the path before he disappears into the back garden.

When he gets home, he makes a cup of tea and sits down to review the photographs he took at the top of Orford castle. The quality of the photos is very good, but Brian does not appear in any of them, even though he knows Brian had been in the view finder when he took them.

Turning to the back of his notebook, where he keeps a list of unanswered questions and mysteries, he adds two more. Why didn't Brian appear in any of the photos and what caused me to have the uneasy feeling outside the nuclear Shelter?

He remembers the last time he felt these feelings, it was during the lead up to the fraud trial and he knows how that turned out.

Suffolk's Last Cold War Victim

Chapter 17

Honesty is the best policy

After an exceptionally tiring morning, trying to work out how to use a washing machine and tumble drier, he sits down and has some lunch. He sits in his armchair, closes his eyes and falls asleep.

At 14:20 pm, his mobile phone's security alarm wakes him up. He checks the screen and sees a tall, blonde woman walking towards the front door. At first he wonders who she is, then quickly realises he's booked a haircut with Andrea today. He has a quick tidy up before answering the door and inviting her in.

He said, 'Hello Andrea, please come in. Would you like a drink before you start?' She replies, 'Yes please Ashley, I'd love a cup of tea, no sugar, please. Would you mind opening the gates so I can drive my car in; I've got all my tools in it?'

He points the remote towards the gates and they begin to swing open. 'You go fetch your car, whilst I make the tea.'

When she re-enters, she asks him which room he wants to use for his hair cut. She said most people chose the kitchen, as it is easier to sweep the hair up on a hard surface afterwards. He agrees and pulls out a breakfast stool to sit on.

'What style would you like?' she asks. 'I'd like a couple of inches off all around please' he replies.

Suffolk's Last Cold War Victim

'I can see your blonde roots are starting to come through. Would you like me to dye them again?' 'Yes please,' he said.

She asks, 'How he are you settling in? He says, 'I really feel at home here and wish I'd done it earlier. How long have you been a hairdresser and when did you go mobile.'

She said, 'I've been doing it since I left school. I served my apprenticeship in a Woodbridge salon for four years. Then eight years ago, I started my own mobile service.' Ashley asks, 'What made you to go out on your own?'

'I loved listening to my customer's gossiping, but in a shop they wouldn't open up as much, as other people could overhear them. When you're mobile, they're in the comfort of their own home and they open up more easily. Wow, you're good. I've never owned up to that before.' She laughs.

Ashley feels at ease with this talkative, confident young lady and asks her a simple question. 'So, who was the villager that cancelled today?'

'Well, the funny thing is, he didn't cancel today, nor did he cancel his appointment four weeks ago today. It's very strange as he always looked forward to me doing his hair. The old bugger always got me with his stories; he's such a wind-up merchant.'

Ashley asks, 'This old man, can you tell me his name?' She says, 'Of course I can, it's not a state secret. His name's Brian Damant.'

Suffolk's Last Cold War Victim

His journalistic mind is going into over-drive. He continues to ask questions, trying not to put her under any pressure. 'Has he ever let you down before?

'Never, if he couldn't make it he'd always phone me.' She said. 'So what happened on that day, four weeks ago today?' asks Ashley.

She reaches into her handbag and pulls out her appointment book. Thumbing through the pages she points to Brian Damant, Tuesday March 28th 14:30 pm.

'It was strange really. I turned up a few minutes before 14:30 pm as normal. I remembered seeing a figure in the front room, as I got out of my car. As I got nearer, I saw it was Peter Hungerford. He was opening and looking into Brian's cupboards and drawers.

He looked up and saw me looking at him. He opened the front door and told me, "Brian's gone to stay with an old friend for a few weeks .He's asked me to look for his address book, so I can cancel his appointments for him." I think there's something really shifty about him. Right Ashley, all done. Anything else I can do for you today?'

She holds up a mirror, so he can see her handiwork. He nods his approval, as she brushes him down and removes the cover before handing him a tissue.

He thanks her for his hair cut and makes another appointment in four weeks time. He does not ask her any more questions regarding Brian's disappearance. He wants to

Suffolk's Last Cold War Victim

speak to Brian first, to confirm if Andrea's version of events is true.

After Andrea drove off, he closed the front gates and went into the kitchen to sweep the hairs off the floor. He feels his head is about to explode with this new information. He mutters, 'I'm picturing Brian and wondering if someone else has been cutting his hair? It's not the length I'd expect it to be after eight weeks growth. Right Ashley, try to relax. Forget this afternoon's revelations and cheer up. You've got a relaxing evening with a lovely lady to look forward to.'

On the way to Laura's house, he stops off at the Co-op to buy six bottles of Ghost Ship. When he arrives outside Laura's house, he feels really nervous for some unknown reason.

At 18:15 pm, he rings the doorbell and waits for her to answer. When she does, the smell of roast beef wafting from the kitchen makes him salivate.

Laura welcomes her guest and ushers him inside. 'I hope you're hungry?' 'I certainly am. I've been busy learning how to operate a washing machine and tumble dryer, so I only had time for a light lunch. Thanks once again for asking me over,' he replies.

She tells him to make himself comfortable in the living room, while she finishes getting the dinner ready. As he looks around the room, he noticed a number of photographs hanging on the walls. Three of them are of Laura and Philip on their wedding day, another two are of an elderly pair, which he presumes are her parents.

Suffolk's Last Cold War Victim

There are also a number of birthday cards on the mantelpiece and windowsill. He calls out to her, 'Laura, are these cards yours?'

'Yes, it was my birthday yesterday.' she states proudly.

'Well happy belated birthday wishes, I wish I'd known I would've sent you a card.'

Laura walks in and fetches two glasses from her drinks' cabinet; she fills them with Ashley's beer. Ten minutes later she invites him into the dining room. She has made him a roast beef dinner with all the trimmings, roast potatoes, carrots, cabbage and a baked suet pudding.

Ashley could not remember the last time a feast like this was laid out before him. He told Laura he hopes it tastes as good as it looks.

After they finished the meal, which turned out to be even better than he had imagined, Ashley offers to do the washing up. She said, 'That's sweet of you to offer, but I'll put it all in the dishwasher later. Let's go back to the sitting room I want to hear how you've been getting on. I'll just go and get the other bottles of beer, so we don't have to keep getting up.'

Ashley glances up to the clock on the wall; it is 19:30 pm. As he is having such a good time, he wishes he can stop the hands moving so fast.

When she comes back in he said, 'Since we last met on Sunday, I've been doing a lot reading and writing. I went for a nice walk to Kelway.' Laura interrupts. 'I've a friend who lives

Suffolk's Last Cold War Victim

in Kelway. Did you use the footpath that goes through the wheat field and meadow?'

'Yes I did, it was beautiful, so quiet and peaceful. Yesterday I visited Orford Castle and heard the tale of the Merman.' Once again Laura excitedly butts in and said, 'I know that one, my Godpop used to tell me that story and he always made me laugh, no matter how many times I heard it.' Ashley loved it when she laughs and the way her shoulders shrug up and down.

Ashley points to a wedding photo and remarks, 'That must be Philip with a beautiful bride by his side?'

'Yes, that's him. He was so proud that day, especially when his family were given special leave to attend the ceremony. He was such a good husband, we were very happy during the time we had together. Did I tell you how he died?'

He said, 'Someone told me about the tragic events surrounding him and Darren, Sarah's husband.'

Laura shocks him when she said, 'Let's get all the horrible, sad news out in the open so we can concentrate on the future. You go first; tell me about your bad bits, but only if you want to. Then I'll tell you mine.'

He wants to tell her the whole truth, but is not sure how much he should reveal. He takes a few moments thinking over this dilemma.

Laura goes over and sits down beside him. She takes hold of his hand and looks into his eyes and tells him, 'When I first lost Philip, I found it hard to talk to anyone about him and the accident. But, after talking to my vicar Michael Moss, the weight started to lift off my shoulders. Perhaps I can help ease your pain as well.'

He nods and begins to explain his predicament. 'What I'm about to tell you, must remain a secret strictly between you, me and these four walls. My life depends on your compliance in this matter.'

Laura, still holding his hand said, 'Ashley, you've my word anything you tell me now, will never be repeated to anyone else, so help me God.'

He begins, 'My real name is George Mitchell; my wife was named Susan and my son, Jason.' He continues telling her how they met, fell in love, married and had a son. They both agree there are similarities with her and Philip's courtship and marriage, except for the son bit. They wanted children, but after three miscarriages they gave up trying.

He explains how he got into journalism and the background to him becoming an investigative journalist. She looks a bit shocked. He said, 'You must be wondering, who the hell is this stranger in my house?' He need not have worried, as she gently squeezes his hand and asks him to continue.

He told her how the fraud investigation came about, starting with the invitation from Mark Haines. How he identified Trevor Bannister and Penka Georgieva's after interviewing their victims. Colonel Hungerford was one of the victims and he is the only person in the village that knows his true identity. He begins croaking when he starts to explain the

Suffolk's Last Cold War Victim

trial, the gang's escape, the assassination of his family and the gang's death threat.

This is why he is now living under a police witness protection scheme and the reason he's had to change his name, appearance and location.

Laura said, 'I remember reading about this story in the newspapers and discussing it with Kat and Glenn in the pub. He'd been following the trial because he heard the Colonel was a victim.

Right I've got two things to ask you, do you feel better now you've shared this with me? And secondly, do you want a refill?'

He replies, 'Laura you can't believe how thankful and relieved I feel now I've shared my story with a new caring friend. And yes please, I'd love a refill, my mouth's really dry.

She pours him another drink and says, 'Thanks for putting your trust in me, I'm so glad there are no secrets between us now. I suggest we say a prayer for our loved ones, then we can talk about things we want to do in the future.' They prayed together before Laura asks, 'So Ashley, what are your plans for the future? '

He said, 'At the moment I'm weighing up all my options. I tend to take each day as it comes. There are still so many things out of my control. If only the police could apprehend the gang I wouldn't be so worried about strangers walking up behind me, or being frightened by unexplained noises in the night.

Suffolk's Last Cold War Victim

Just talking and being with you tonight has made me feel both happy and sad at the same time. Sad, because I loved sitting and talking to Susan about things we'd done that day. And happy because you've taken me back to those good times. I'm so glad I moved to this village. The people are so kind and welcoming, especially my present company.

I've been doing some research on the Suffolk dialect and I've a friend who's trying to get me Suffolkated. I still love writing and I've lots of ideas for a novel about a fictional Suffolk village. That's me done what about you?'

Laura takes a while before she says, 'In 2011 I lost both my parents within three months of each other. This was three years before Philip's untimely death. I've been widowed for nearly four years now, but recently I've been feeling incredibly lonely.

My only company has been my pupils, Sarah, Kat, Glenn and my Godpop Brian. As I listened to you just now, I realise we're both in the same boat, trying to make the best of each day. I too have enjoyed your company; I do hope we can continue being friends. The one thing I've learnt is, we may have lost our loved ones physically, but we'll never lose our love for them.'

Glancing up to the clock again, he sees it is nearly 22:30 pm. 'I see it's getting late and I don't want to outstay my visit, knowing you've got school tomorrow.' She looks up to make sure he's not misread the time and hoping he can stay a little longer. But he's not mistaken, so has to agree with him, it's time to call it a night.

Suffolk's Last Cold War Victim

At the front door, he asks Laura if he can provide her with a meal and show her around his house on Friday evening. He was careful not to say he would be the one cooking it. Laura put her arms around him and gives him a big hug. As he leaves he said 'Cheerio tegither.'

He cannot remember the walk home; he is so happy, something he never thought he would feel again.

Suffolk's Last Cold War Victim

Chapter 18

Where's Jamie Oliver when you want him?

When the alarm clock wakes him in the morning, he is a bit miffed as he was still dreaming of being with Laura last night. A sudden pang of guilt comes over him. He mutters, 'If Laura made an effort to cook me a meal, I should do the same. But where do I start? I've never had to cook a meal from scratch before. There's only one thing for it, go online.'

He spends the next hour searching the internet looking for a menu he can cook for Laura. He remembers seeing some cookbooks in Sarah's shop; perhaps she can point him in the right direction.

At the shop he explains his dilemma to her. She thinks it's rather sweet of him to go to all this trouble. She said, 'If I were you, I'd go the Co-op and buy one of their 'Cook in the Bag' chickens, a bag of Maris Piper potatoes, a few carrots and a bag of frozen peas. For dessert, go for her favourite, a sticky toffee pudding with custard.

Make sure you read and follow the cooking instructions precisely for a delicious chicken. Peel and chop the potatoes and carrots. If you've got a steamer put the potatoes in the saucepan, cover them with water. In the steamer pan add the carrots and frozen peas, place this on top of the saucepan with the lid on it. Boil the potatoes until you

Suffolk's Last Cold War Victim

can easily push a knife through them. It normally takes between twenty to twenty-five minutes.

When the potatoes are cooked, empty some of the water into another small saucepan with some gravy mix. Drain the remaining water from the potatoes, add some butter, and a pinch of salt before mashing them. Heat a couple of plates before serving the meal.

The pudding can be cooked in a microwave oven. The custard comes in a sachet and only needs boiling water added to it, plus plenty of stirring to stop it going lumpy. Remember, follow the instructions on the labels and you will be fine.'

He thanks Sarah for her suggestions and promises to let her know how it goes on Saturday evening.

In the Co-op he buys two of everything, he wants to have a practice run later this evening. Until then, he spends all his time vacuuming, dusting, cleaning the windows and ironing the washing from yesterday.

He set a timer to go off at 19:30 pm. The time he plans to have dinner ready tomorrow evening. He shocks himself when the dinner is not only ready at the desired time, it is also very tasty.

He spends the rest of the evening trying to make sense of the mysteries in the back of his notebook. Some of the answers he came up with are dismissed. They may have made sense, if they were not so far-fetched.

Friday morning starts very early, as he is woken by the squawking of two magpies in the back garden. He looks out of

Suffolk's Last Cold War Victim

his bedroom window and sees the bird's dive bombing a fox on his lawn. They did not give up, until they had seen off the fox and the danger it posed to their young.

Still marvelling at the bravery of the birds he mutters, 'That grass is getting long, I'll give it a cut today.'

He worries he's not seen Brian for a few days. He decides to go and look for him this afternoon. In the meantime, he finds his lawnmower in the garage and sets about cutting his lawn.

After a light lunch he goes to Brian's house, knocking on the door proved fruitless, he wonders if he has gone to visit Maggie's grave. In the well-maintained graveyard, he starts to search for her headstone.

He had been looking for about ten minutes when he found a headstone with the names of John and Sylvia Orris carved into it. Looking down, it read "Beloved parents of Laura."

Continuing to look around, he spots two more headstones which bore the names of Allen Damant, died March 1993 and Agatha Damant died September 1993, he presumed these were Brian's parents.

Directly opposite his parents' grave, he finds what he is looking for. Here is the headstone of Brian's wife, Margaret. He's a bit surprised about the condition of her grave.

There is a pot of dead flowers hanging limply over the sides. He knows Brian visited her grave when he dropped him off last Tuesday, following their trip to Ipswich. The decayed

Suffolk's Last Cold War Victim

flowers look as if they have been here for a number of weeks. He wonders why Brian had not thrown them away.

Having found no trace of his friend, he decides to return home to get ready to cook for his visitor this evening.

Ashley cannot decide whether to use the chicken left over from yesterday's trial run or cook a fresh bird. He says to himself, 'It's a no brainer you idiot, use the fresh option you don't want to poison her.'

He set the timers to 19:20 pm giving him ten minutes to dish up for 19:30 pm. Laura arrives on time at 18:30, setting off the security alarm he forgot to turn off.

He takes her coat and hangs it up in the cupboard next to the front door. He says, 'Welcome to my humble abode. I hope you're hungry and you like chicken?'

She replies, 'I'm so sorry, but I've an allergy to white meat.' He's gobsmacked and wants the ground to swallow him up, before getting the courage to look at her. When he does, he sees her shoulders shrugging up and down and hears her burst into hysterical laughter. 'I'm so sorry Ashley, I bumped into Sarah earlier, she told me what you're preparing for dinner. As you've discovered, I love a wind up with my friends and seeing their reactions. I've got to say, seeing your face was priceless.'

He sees the funny side and takes it in good faith, as he does with another wind-up merchant he knows.

They chat about their day whilst drinking a glass of their favourite tipple. The timers go off, signalling it is time for

Suffolk's Last Cold War Victim

him to go and dish up. He's been in the kitchen for five minutes when there is an almighty crash of saucepans and a desperate cry of 'Oh no' from Ashley.

Laura immediately dashes into the kitchen to help her friend, only to find two plates of delicious food laid out on a table on the dining table. 'Gotcha' he exclaims. He can tell by the look on her face, she enjoyed this moment as much as he did.

Laura compliments Ashley on his culinary skills, especially her favourite, the sticky toffee pudding and custard. She asks if she can help him with the washing up. He tells her, 'As you're my guest I want you to relax and I'll clear it up later, just as you told me on Wednesday.

He gives her a tour of the house, pointing out the rooms he wants to redecorate. She offers to help him choose some new curtains, bed sheets and carpets, if he wants. He told her he would welcome her input in these matters. He admits he's not good with colour coordination and how he left that sort of thing to Susan.

At the end of the evening, he asks, 'As its dark and getting late, I'd like to walk you home so I know you're safe. She gracefully accepts the offer, as it meant they can have some extra minutes together. Before they leave, Ashley asks her if she wants any of the left chicken. She said, 'Why don't I take it all and make you a curry?' He did not need asking twice. He quickly puts the chicken in a large Tupperware carton and gives it to her. He cannot wait to taste it.

Suffolk's Last Cold War Victim

Delivering her safely to her door, Laura thanks him for a lovely evening and said she looks forward to seeing him in the pub tomorrow evening. He replies, 'I'm looking forward to that too. By the way, two good friends of mine, Mark and Craig are coming to stay with me on Sunday evening. I'd love to introduce them to you, if you are free.'

She said, 'I'd like that, I can put faces to the names I heard you talking about on Wednesday. After another hug, this time a bit longer and tighter, they said their goodbyes.

On the way home he passes Brian's house, the curtains are still wide open. He remembers Brian telling him, people must be mad leaving their curtains open when its dark, if the lights are on anyone walking by, can see what is going on inside. At least the lights are not on.

The last thing he can remember doing this night was to tell his family, 'Guys you'll never believe what I did today.'

Suffolk's Last Cold War Victim

Chapter 19

Some furrener's want to meet you

He spends Saturday morning shopping for his guests' full English breakfast on Monday. Popping into Sarah's shop, he thanks her for all her help in organising the meal for Laura last night. 'I am really looking forward to meeting you all again this evening.' She said, 'I'm pleased to have been a help.'

Arriving home, he goes through the evidence he is going to present to his friends tomorrow, starting with the fraudulent Property Developer, Steve Rogers. He has a list of people, who have taken money for information or passed planning permission for his company. The list also contains dates, locations and the amount of money involved. The one omission from the list will be Colin Scott; Ashley has already planned his comeuppance.

He will show them the recording from the pub, to prove the type of things Rogers has been doing to get his planning applications passed. He is only doing this as he is worried how Craig will react to these accusations, based on the hearsay of Brian alone.

The next case involves the deliberate spiking of Melvin Gale's drink in a Woodbridge nightclub. Once again, he wonders if it will be taken seriously, as it is another case of hearsay.

Suffolk's Last Cold War Victim

In the pub in the evening, he's pleased to see the gang again. As he makes his way to their table, he overhears someone on a table opposite say, 'This is the longest time Brian's ever been away from the village'. From what he is hearing, they all seem to be concerned for his welfare. Ashley wishes he could put their concerns to rest and tell them he has been in regular contact with him.

During the karaoke session, Laura got Ashley to join her on stage. They sang Sonny and Cher's hit, 'I've got you babe.' As it happens, they got the biggest cheer of the night from an appreciative crowd.

The next morning, he has no problem getting up and getting to the Church service on time. Listening to the service, he suddenly realises it has only been a few weeks since the deaths of his family. In these ten short weeks, which seems like eight months, so much has happened.

He wonders what Susan and Jason would think of the new cottage, the village and his friendship with Laura. He hopes they know how much he misses them both, but he needs to keep himself busy and to be with other people for the sake of his mental health.

After the service finished, he asks Laura if she is still coming to meet his friends. She said she looks forward to it and would be round at 18:00 pm.

Just before 15:30 pm, Ashley's phone rings. It's Mark Haines, asking him to open the gates as they are about to turn into his road.

Suffolk's Last Cold War Victim

He is really pleased to see his friends again; they too are pleased and also impressed by his cheery demeanour. Once inside, Ashley takes them upstairs to their bedrooms. Mark has stayed previously, but this is the first time Craig has been to the cottage or the village.

Craig said, 'I'm so glad you've settled in so quickly. You're looking very well I must say. Here's a little something for you,' he hands him a bottle of his favourite, single malt whisky. Ashley thanks his friend for the kind gift and tells them there are drinks and snacks in the kitchen.

They are very grateful as they drove nonstop all the way here. Ashley said, 'Right, we'll have these while we're having a catch up.'

Craig is sorry to report the police are no nearer locating the gang's whereabouts. Mark adds the paper will continue printing pictures of the gang in the hope someone will recognise them and come forward to claim the reward.

Ashley thanks them both for keeping his tragedy in the public spotlight. He said, 'Right, now it's my turn. As I told you both on the phone, I've evidence on Colin Scott and Steve Rogers, a businessman whose been bribing council officials to get his planning proposals passed. I've names, addresses and the building sites involved.

I'm now going to show you a recording I took of one such meeting in the Belford Arms last Saturday week.'

As they watch the ten-minute recording, Ashley looks at their faces. Craig is listening intently to every word, Mark is

Suffolk's Last Cold War Victim

smiling and rubbing his hands, a sure sign he thinks he has a headline story that will make him a lot of money. When it is over, Craig asks how he knew when and where to place the camera.

'My source is a local man, who I first met last year when I interviewed Colonel Hungerford. He told me the exact time and table it was going to happen on. He's told me another meeting is scheduled for Tuesday evening at a pub in Ipswich. Rogers is being frustrated by an elderly lady, who refuses to sell him part of her land. He's going to hire a thug to make her life a misery until she agrees to sell it to him.

If you use surveillance equipment, similar to mine you'll get enough evidence to open a full investigation into his fraudulent dealings. The rest of the information he's given me is also hearsay I'm afraid.

There's another thing I thought you should know; he's a client of Barry Colson. Perhaps he might provide some information in exchange for an even easier time in prison.'

Craig asked, 'Do you think your man would be prepared to give us a statement?' Mark chips in, 'That goes for me too.'

Ashley said, 'I'll ask the next time I see him. May I remind you of the caveat I insisted on earlier. The men in the recording are Steve Rogers, a Property Developer, and Colin Scott, the husband of Nicola Scott, a Conservative, East Suffolk Councillor and Chairperson of the Planning Committee. I don't want you to pursue him; I've got a plan to punish him without implicating his wife, and also benefit the village.'

Suffolk's Last Cold War Victim

Both friends said in unison, 'How?' Ashley continues, 'I know he's got fifty grand hidden in a safe at his home, his wife is unaware of the safe and its contents. He's collected the money over the past years from people like Rogers.

I've made a copy of the recording and a letter which I'll be posting to him. It'll say, I'll send this evidence to the police if he doesn't donate the money anonymously, to the Belford village youth clubhouse appeal.'

Mark is gobsmacked by the simplicity of Ashley's proposed reparations for Scott and wishes he can write about it in his newspaper.

Ashley explains the second crime that's about to take place. 'Some teenage boys from a nearby village are preparing to spike the drink of Melvin Gale, a Belford villager, on Friday 4th May, in the Bandbox nightclub in Woodbridge.

They're hoping to disgrace Melvin for taking a girlfriend away from one of them. He's also the son of their former Headmaster at Framlingham high school. I've got descriptions of the three young men involved.

I know Melvin's parents, they're really decent people. Neither he, nor his parents deserve this kind of thing happening to them.'

Craig said, 'I know a DCI in this area, I'll give him a call later this evening. We're getting a lot of pressure to crack down on this type of crime. On the Rogers case, I'll give my governor a call first thing tomorrow morning. He doesn't like being disturbed on a Sunday.

Suffolk's Last Cold War Victim

You say you got all this from a villager? How the hell did he manage to get all this info? I'd give my right arm to have an informer, like him working for me.'

Mark's grinning as he looks at Ashley and says, 'You tell your mate, if he doesn't want to be a police informant, I'll give him a job on my paper. I've still got a vacancy since I lost my last investigator earlier this year.'

Craig goes into another room to ring his fellow DCI. When he has finished, he comes back to his friends and finds a nice pint of 'Ghost Ship' waiting for him. He said, 'My colleagues pleased with the intelligence and hopes these are the same yobs who've been spiking drinks in the area over the last few months.

Craig asks Ashley to tell him a bit more about the old man. He takes a large swig of beer and says, 'Where do I start? Well I first met Brian last year, when I came here to interview Colonel Hungerford. I loved his Suffolk accent and trying to decipher what he was saying. He remembered meeting me last year when I was called George; I haven't told him my new name's Ashley.

He's been helping me to become Suffolkated. He was a postman, working his entire career in the area before his retirement. He's the biggest wind-up merchant I've ever known. I promise when you meet him, you'll like him too.

His information on the villagers, especially the dubious ones has been spot on. But I've got so many unanswered mysteries surrounding him; I don't know where to start to solve them.'

Suffolk's Last Cold War Victim

Mark wants to hear about some of these mysteries. 'OK, now you've whetted our appetite, give us a taster.'

Ashley said, 'Well, you asked. He supposedly told the Colonel's son Peter, he was going to stay with a friend in Bury St Edmunds for a few weeks. No one has seen him since, except me. He regularly visits me, which is how I got the information I gave you earlier.

Even when we've been talking together in public, people look at me as if I'm talking to myself.

He can enter my garden without activating the security alarms. He's always wearing the same clothes, each time I see him, regardless of the weather conditions. He never eats or drinks in my presence.

People in the village, especially his oldest friends, are starting to worry about his absence from the village. I've seen Peter Hungerford acting suspiciously when I saw him leaving Brian's house. If I hadn't been talking to Brian, I'd report his absence to the police myself.

I tried recording some of his stories on my voice recorder the other day. When I played it back, I heard my voice and background noises, but nothing from Brian. I also took some photographs from the top of Orford castle, but when I came to review them, I found he was nowhere to be seen. Hopefully, I'll be able to introduce him to you during your stay.'

Suffolk's Last Cold War Victim

Just then, the doorbell rings. 'That's probably Laura. I'll just go and let her in.' Leaving the room he hears his friends whispering. He wonders what they are talking about.

'Hi Laura, please come in and I'll introduce you to my friends.' They enter the living room, 'Laura these are my good friends Mark and Craig. Guys, this is my very dear, new friend, Laura Archibald.'

They both welcome Laura, without letting on how they know Ashley. They had agreed beforehand if the question came up, they would say they worked with him in the Civil Service. Little did they know, Ashley had already told her the full story a few days ago?

They continue talking for another forty minutes or so, before Ashley said, Right guys I don't know about you but I'm feeling hungry. Laura would you like to join us in the pub? She said, 'I'd loved to, but I've got to prepare next week lessons.

As they leave for the pub, Ashley tells his mates to carry on while he makes sure Laura gets home safely. After a big hug, he tell her his friends will be going home on Tuesday morning and to give him a call if she wants some company during the week.

He'd only taken a few steps towards the pub when he heard Brian say, 'Whoop George...heow're yoo diddl'n? Oy need ter see yoo as soon as poss.'

He says, 'Great to see you Brian, I'm glad you're here. I've got some friends staying with me and they'd love to meet

Suffolk's Last Cold War Victim

you. You're quite welcome to join us in the pub, or you can come round tomorrow.'

Brian said he would pass on the invitation to the pub, but will see him later as he had something important he needs to tell him. As he walks off, Ashley mutters, 'He's done it again. 'I've another mystery to add to the list.'

When Ashley joins his friends in the pub they all agree, as it has been a long day they would only have a couple of drinks with their meal, before going home to chill out.

Suffolk's Last Cold War Victim

Chapter 20

Only a few people have the gift

They arrive home just after nine o'clock. Ashley goes into the kitchen to get some beer from the fridge. Looking out of the window he sees Brian, sitting on a bench under the moonlight in his garden. He unlocks the back door and asks him to come inside.

Mark and Craig are seated in the lounge as Ashley led Brian into the room. Ashley full of pride announces, 'Listen guys, you asked to see Brian, well here he is.' Ashley points to Brian as he sits down on a chair in the corner of the room.

Mark asks, 'What are we supposed to be looking at?' 'I told you, this is my friend Brian Damant,' replies Ashley, feeling a bit embarrassed by Mark's comment.

His mates look at each other, not really knowing what to say or do. Craig looked at Mark and mimes, "It's a 'Wind-Up.' After a long pause, it's Brian who speaks first. 'George, you need to sit down then, I'll tell you why I'm here and why your friends can't see me.'

Ashley slumps down on his sofa next to Craig. Brian continues, 'George, I want you to repeat verbatim everything I'm about to say, it's the only way your friends will know what's going on. I need you to explain why they can't see or

Suffolk's Last Cold War Victim

hear me, but you can. If they want to ask me any questions, all they have to do is ask. Nod if you understand.'

He nods his head, before Brian continues, 'Tell them what I've just said.'

'Guys I don't know what's going on here, I'm as mystified as you are, so please let's see how this plays out. Brian's asked me to repeat his words to you. He said, you can ask him as many questions as you like.'

Brian asked Ashley to contact Laura and ask her to come round to listen to what he has to say, as it involves her too. He replies, as it was getting late, she may not want to come round.

'Please call her as I don't know how much longer I've got left.' Ashley senses the seriousness of the situation and rings her right away. When she answers he said, 'Hi Laura, I'm so sorry to call you this late, but someone wants you to hear his story, can you please come round as soon as possible. This isn't a wind-up, I promise you.'

She too, senses something is not right and said she would be round in ten minutes.

Brian begins talking, with Ashley repeating his words. 'George, you must be wondering why you're the only person that's seen me in many a week.

It's because you've got a gift not many people have. You have the ability to communicate with spirits that have suffered a sudden tragic death. These spirits, of which I'm one, are stuck in a form of limbo. We can't go back, nor can we

Suffolk's Last Cold War Victim

fully pass on until, we and our loved ones get some form of closure.

You've had your suspicions for some time, that things didn't quite add up and you're right. When Laura gets here, I'll explain everything. In the meantime, I've two small pieces of trivia I hope will convince Mark and Craig this isn't a wind-up.

Mark, just before Craig picked you up today, you spilt a cup of tea down the front of your shirt. You put another shirt on that hadn't been ironed.

Craig, when you left home today, you remembered you hadn't locked the back door and had to return home to lock it. I'm sure you want to talk together about my observations while we wait for Laura.'

Ashley looks at them; they did not have to say anything, as the look of utter amazement on their faces said it all. Just to be sure, Ashley asked, 'Guys, was Brian correct?' Still unable to speak, they both just nodded.

When the doorbell rang, Ashley got up to let Laura in. Before they go into the lounge, he said, 'Laura, I'm so sorry for calling you like that, but I swear on my life, this isn't a wind-up and it's nothing to do with the alcohol we've had tonight.

We've a visitor who's asked me to repeat his words for him. Apparently, I'm the only one who can see or hear him. He believes I've got the gift of a clairvoyant. Tell me what you think before we go in.'

Laura takes hold of his hand and says, 'I can only say I believe things happen, that can't easily be explained away.

Suffolk's Last Cold War Victim

You've always been truthful with me, so I'm going to keep an open mind.'

When they enter the room, she sees the men's ashen faces apparently staring into space. Still unable to speak they just nod to welcome her. Both men have pens and paper ready to record Brian's narratives. Laura takes a seat in an airchair.

Brian begins again, 'My story begins on the morning of Wednesday 28th April. I was in my house having a cup of tea with Peter Hungerford, my gardener. He asked me what I was doing for the rest of the day. I told him Andrea's coming to cut my hair in the afternoon and I needed a birthday card from the Co-op. I also wanted to check my euro lottery ticket from the night before as well.

He told me he can check my ticket with an app he has on his mobile phone. He scanned the ticket and showed me the screen with the winning numbers. As I hadn't won anything I screwed it up and threw it in the bin.

He said he drove me to the shops, if I helped him with a job he's doing for his dad. When I asked what it was, he said, "He's writing a book about an old nuclear shelter and he wants me to take some photos inside it."

I told him to come back in twenty minutes, as I had a few chores to do. Twenty minutes later, he picked me up. As we drove off he told me, "On the way I'm going to a hardware shop in Woodbridge to buy a big torch to light up the shelter."

Suffolk's Last Cold War Victim

That worked well for me as there's a good card shop in the town. When we both got what we wanted, he drove on towards Eyke. We arrived at the Shelter, the one I showed you on Tuesday.'

Ashley says, 'So that's why you asked me if I could find the place again.' Continuing, Brian said, 'Yes, and do you remember saying, you had a feeling something bad had happened there?

Anyway, he lifted a large rusty door and helped me down the steps into the shelter. He cut his hand on a rusty metal handrail causing little drops of his blood to fall onto the floor.

He passed me the torch to hold up, whilst he took the photos. He started cursing when he realised he'd left the camera in the car. "Brian, I'm just going back to the car to fetch the camera."

All of a sudden, I heard a large crashing sound as the door closed. I thought the door had been caught by a gust of wind causing it to close. I wasn't worried as I knew Peter would be back very soon.

But he didn't come back soon; in fact, he never came back at all. He'd locked the door, by wedging a metal rod in a loop, where a padlock would have gone. I was trapped in a fifteen by ten-foot, airtight room. There was a door at the far end, which I presumed led into the main area. I tried to get in, but it was locked. That's when I started to panic; I only had this torch for lighting. I didn't know which would deplete first, the torch batteries or the oxygen in the room.

Suffolk's Last Cold War Victim

Peter, the little bugger, went straight back to my house, he knew where I kept my spare house key. He was looking for the euro ticket I'd thrown away earlier. He knew I hadn't won anything on the lottery numbers, but I had won one million pounds on the winning codes.

Unknown to him, I'd taken the ticket from the bin. I use the same numbers each week copying the numbers off the old ticket and he's been looking for it ever since. That's why he's been acting suspiciously in front of you and Andrea. He invented the story of me going away.

I'd been in this horrible dark, damp hellhole for two days, when a disgusting smell became overpowering.' Craig, who is listening intently as the story unfolds asks, 'This smell, was it because of the dampness or the oxygen being depleted?' Brian's answer makes Ashley laugh out loud, before he composes himself and continues, 'No, it's because I'd had a couple or three craps.'

This time it was Laura who interrupts and said, 'This man you're talking about, is it my Godpop, Brian Damant? If it is, I believe everything he's just said. Only he would make a joke in the middle of all this sadness.'

Brian begins again, 'That's me alright; it was your birthday card I bought, and you thought I'd forgotten to send you one. I realised time was running out for me, so I wrote Laura's name and address on the back of the ticket. On the card, I've written the whole story of the pact me and Maggie made with your parents for your conception. I also wrote down the code to my safe, which has a copy of my will, leaving

Suffolk's Last Cold War Victim

everything I own to you. It's behind a picture of you in my living room. I've placed the card and lottery ticket in an envelope and hid it on a shelf in the far corner. I hid it, just in case he came back to search for the ticket.

Anyway, to cut a long story short, sometime on day two or three, the air finally ran out and I died. Craig, forensics will find his blood and fingerprints inside the bunker, CCTV from the hardware store will show Peter buying the torch and his mobile phone records will show he was at the location on that day, I heard him talking to his dad just as we arrived.'

Ashley asked Brian for a short break. He needs a drink and wants to ask his guests for their thoughts so far.

Laura is the first to speak. She wants to know what he meant regarding her conception and does Ashley know anything about this. He asks the others to excuse them, before taking her into the kitchen to discuss what he knows.

He takes his notebook with him. He finds the page he wrote the story of how Brian and Maggie helped a couple in the village to conceive a baby.

As his notes were written in shorthand, he suggests he reads it out, but she tells him she can read it herself as she also uses shorthand.

A few minutes later she realises Ashley is telling the truth. Nowhere in the story does it mention the little girl's name. As she's never told him her maiden name is Orris, how can he have known that she's Brian's biological daughter.

Suffolk's Last Cold War Victim

She asks, 'Can I please have a cuddle?' Ashley obliges and pulls her close; he feels her body shaking uncontrollably, as she nestles in his arms. The shaking eases off, but he still holds her close for a few more minutes.

She backs away and tells him, 'I need to call my Headmaster to let him know, I won't be in tomorrow.' He asks if she wants a glass of beer. She asks, 'Do you have anything stronger? '

Ashley remembers Craig's present and says, 'I've a bottle of single malt whisky or I'll go out and get you something'. She said the whisky would be perfect.

He asks, 'Can you remember telling me, you took after your father in liking Ghost ship, before correcting yourself saying he drank lager. How right you were first time.'

Ashley asks the boys if they want a glass of whisky. Craig and Mark said they would prefer a cup of black coffee, sensing it's going to be a long night ahead. When Ashley brings the drinks through, he looks at Brian. He has his thumbs up and said, 'Good boy.'

Trying to make sense of the situation Ashley asks each one what they make of the revelations. Craig said he would kick off first. 'I've heard stories of this kind of thing happening before when a clairvoyant was asked to help provide a breakthrough in cases that had hit an impasse.

I've always been a bit sceptical on the subject, until today when he told you about me having to return home to

Suffolk's Last Cold War Victim

lock my back door. If you were winding us up, how could you've known about this detail?

From the evidence we've heard using DNA analysis, we can prove he's been in the shelter. We can also put him in the vicinity by using mobile phone data. The one thing we can't prove is his motive. We only have Brian's account of the lottery ticket theory, and we can't call him as a witness. What if he'd found the ticket right away? He may have gone back and released Brian, but we'll never know.

The best we can do is to catch him going back into the shelter, finding the ticket and trying to claim the prize. If he did that, we may be able to get a conviction.'

Mark agrees with Craig's sentiments adding, 'If we ran the lottery ticket theory in our paper based on Brian's story, we'd be the laughingstock of our competitors.

Laura will still be able to collect the lottery winnings. If Camelot asks how she got the ticket, she can answer truthfully, it's a birthday present from her 'Godpop'. As for the delay in claiming the prize, she can say she'd mislaid it for a while.

If he was caught in the act, it would make headlines in our paper. Otherwise it's a story of an elderly man who died in an abandoned nuclear shelter, left over from the Cold War with the Soviet Union.'

Brian asks if he can continue. Ashley nods and asked his guests to pick up their pens and notebooks. 'Right George, I've been joined by three other spirits who're desperate to

Suffolk's Last Cold War Victim

pass on some information to you all. The first one goes by the name of ...'

Ashley heard the name but couldn't believe what he is hearing. Laura asks, 'Who is it Ashley, what's the spirit's name?'

'It's "my little Trojan horse", my pet name for Susan.' Brian continues, 'She has some information on the location of the gang responsible for her and Jason's murders.

They're holed up at a remote farmhouse in Cambridgeshire. On Wednesday afternoon, all five members of the gang, together with their horde of £1.2 million in cash, will be driven to Cambridge airport. Posing as property developers, they've chartered a private jet to fly them to Palma airport in Majorca. From there they'll split into two pairs and one single. Using false passports they'll go on separate flights to their final destination, the Dominican Republic.

The money will be collected and laundered by contacts of Penka Georgieva's family. The clean money will be deposited into five new Swiss bank accounts, ready for them to transfer over whenever they need it.'

Craig asked for the full address, which he carefully writes down. He said, 'I don't care what my boss say's about being disturbed on a Sunday, he's going to want to hear this. We must start preparing for their arrests immediately.' He and Mark go into different rooms to make some phone calls.

Suffolk's Last Cold War Victim

Ashley asks Brian, 'If I' a clairvoyant why can't I hear or see Susan and Jason.' Brian answers, 'On very rare occasions, some can see their loved ones. Remember your boat trip on Lake Windermere?' He replies, 'I knew it was them. You said there were three spirits, who's the third?'

Brian said, 'The third spirit is called "Cushion".' Ashley said, I don't know anyone named Cushion.'

'I do', said Laura, 'That's what I called Philip. When we were watching the telly, I used to lay my head on his belly for a cushion.'

Brian continues, 'They've told me to tell you this. "We love you both with all our hearts, but we've gone. We believe you're made for each other and we'd love to see your relationship blossom. Now we've expressed our feelings, we're hopeful we can find closure on our final journey. You must never feel guilty about your feelings for each other." Brian waits for a few minutes before saying, 'They've all gone through the door to be reunited, with their long lost relatives. They're the lucky ones; I wish I could join them.'

Laura is the first to speak. 'What on earth's happening here? I'm having trouble keeping up with my emotions. I don't want to be alone tonight, can I stay here, please?' Ashley tells her, 'I'm feeling exactly the same way. By the look of things, nobody in the house will be getting much sleep tonight anyway.

Craig comes back into the room, buzzing with excitement. 'My boss has just called me back after talking to

Suffolk's Last Cold War Victim

the Assistant Commissioner. He's given me full control of the operation to apprehend the gang.

Tomorrow morning, I've got to report to Martlesham Police HQ and brief a senior officer on Brian's case. While I'm there I'll give my mate more details of the drink spiking.

I just wish Peter Hungerford would simply own up to his crime. It would certainly make things a lot easier for everybody.

As we speak, the fraud squad are getting a team together to investigate Steve Rogers' Company. The boss is also considering the Colson route, it may save a lot of time and money if he cooperates.'

Mark was next to give an update. 'Ashley, will you be my investigative journalist on the Rogers case?' The look on Ashley's face said it all. 'Thought not, but I had to ask.

Our sister paper, 'Everyday News' will have reporters in place to get exclusives on all the revelations. I've got them to agree not to film or interview anyone from the village, without my express permission. This'll help to keep your cover intact.

Craig and I have agreed to cooperate with each other to obtain evidence. Laura, we're so sorry for the loss of your Godfather. From what we've heard from Ashley, it sounds like he was quite a character.' She thanks them for their kind words and looks forward to a swift conclusion to all these crimes.

Suffolk's Last Cold War Victim

Ashley announces, 'As it's now 01:30 am and Brian has gone, I think it's time to get some sleep. I've a feeling it's going to be even more hectic tomorrow.

They all agree with him and retire to their bedrooms, except Ashley and Laura. They settle down on the sofa, cuddling up to each other. Laura is the first to fall asleep. Ashley is thinking about something Craig said earlier. "I just wish Peter Hungerford would simply own up to his crime. "

Suddenly he sits up and whispers to himself, 'That's it; I know exactly who I need to talk to tomorrow.' Only after his eureka moment can he close his eyes and fall asleep.

Suffolk's Last Cold War Victim

Chapter 21

A village in shock

Laura is the first to rise, trying hard not to wake Ashley. She stands up and looks at him; his eyes are still shut, she bends over and kisses him lightly on his forehead.

The smell of fresh coffee permeating through the house, stirs the men from their slumber. It is not long before they all join her in the kitchen.

Craig asks, 'Yesterday, was it just a dream, or did it really happen?'

Ashley answers, 'It was all real I'm afraid. What time do you have to be at Martlesham HQ?' He replies, 'I've got to be there at 08:00 am. I still did not know how I'm going to explain how I obtained the evidence.'

Mark asks Ashley if he will give him a lift to Ipswich Railway station, so he can catch a train to London. He wants to liaise with the editor of Everyday News in his office. Ashley asks, 'What times your train?' Mark says, 'I hope to catch the 12:09 pm, so 11:45 am would be ideal'. Ashley said, 'That'll work well as this'll give me enough time to speak to a man about a gardener.'

After breakfast, Craig left for Martlesham HQ. Mark makes a number of phone calls to his office. Laura's going

Suffolk's Last Cold War Victim

home for a change of clothing before meeting Ashley again in the afternoon.

Ashley walks the few hundred yards to the home of Colonel Hungerford. When he arrives at the house, he is relieved Peter's van is not in the driveway. He rings the bell, praying someone is at home.

The door is opened by the man himself. 'Hello Ashley, how are you, old boy? Come in, I've just made you a pot of tea.'

The Colonel brings in the pot of tea and a plate of biscuits placing them on a table between two armchairs He asks, 'Now what can I do for you?'

Ashley said, 'I'm so sorry to bring this to your door, I hardly know where to begin.' The Colonel, looking a bit anxious said, 'The gangs not on to you are they?'

'No sir, that's not it. What I have to say is a lot worse than that. Anyway here goes. Can you remember Mark Haines, the editor of the World of News and Craig Ferguson, the DCI in the fraud trial?' He nods his head to acknowledge he remembers them.

'Well, they've been staying with me over the weekend. Yesterday they received some information on the disappearance of Brian Damant.'

'But he's not missing he's staying with friends in Bury St, Edmunds. If you talk to Peter, he'll tell you,' said the Colonel.

Suffolk's Last Cold War Victim

Ashley says, 'I really wish this was true, unfortunately there's another explanation. The police have reason to believe Peter's a major suspect in the disappearance and possible murder of Brian. They'll be searching an area near Eyke, where they believe they'll find his body, together with Peter's blood and fingerprints. I thought you should be given a chance to talk to him first. If it's true, the best thing for him would be to hand himself in to the police.'

The poor man did not answer for a few minutes, as he tries to process this information. Eventually he asks, 'How long before the police will be knocking on the door?' Ashley says, 'I can't give you an exact time, but I think it will be later this afternoon.

'I'm really sorry to be the bearer of bad news. I've a lot of respect for you and your wife and I'd hate to see the police breaking down your doors to arrest your son. Can I leave it with you to have a word with him?

'You can definitely leave it with me. Trust me he'll be doing the right thing, even if I have to drag him to the police station myself. Thanks for giving me the heads up on this one.'

On the walk home Ashley is joined by Brian. 'Hello Brian, I thought you'd be long gone by now.' 'Ho! That doon't werk loike 'at...Oy'm still troy'n ter werk 'at owt,' he replied.

Ashley asks Brian to double check if Susan, Jason and Philip have managed to go to their final resting places. Brian confirms they have, but there is still something stopping him from crossing over and joining them.

Suffolk's Last Cold War Victim

He had been home for forty minutes, when he receives a phone call from the Colonel. 'Ashley, it's the Colonel here. I thought I'd let you know how I got on with my son. After I confronted him with your evidence he broke down in tears, before telling me exactly what he'd done and his motive for doing it. Do the police know about the euro lottery ticket?' Ashley has to lie and pleads ignorance on the subject. The Colonel continues, 'He told me wanted to use the winnings to replace the money we lost in the fraud.

Anyway, right now he's on the way to the police station to confess. I was getting ready to go with him, but he's gone off without me. If your policeman friend hears anything, can you please let me know right away?'

Ashley said he would and is pleased he has done the right thing. He rings Craig immediately to tell him the good news regarding Peter Hungerford. His phone is constantly engaged, so he leaves a message on Craig's voice mail.

Mark comes downstairs with his luggage and loads it in the car boot, ready for his lift to the station. 'Peter's on his way to the police station to confess everything, including the lottery ticket motive' said Ashley.

Mark exclaims, 'What made him do that?' Ashley said, 'I went to see the Colonel earlier and told him the whole story. He managed to convince Peter to hand himself in to the police.'

On the way to the station they talk about life after the gang's capture. Will he remain in the village, revert to his

Suffolk's Last Cold War Victim

original name, and resume his journalist career? Ashley answers, 'Yes, no, no'

Standing outside the station having waved his friend off, he feels pins and needles piercing his head. Is this another harbinger that something bad has happened? Should he try and stop Mark getting on the train, or has something happened in the village and did it involve Laura?

He remembers Laura is meeting him later this afternoon, so decides to go home in case he misses her. Everything looks normal as he arrives home. As he puts his key in the door, he hears his phone ringing. He had forgotten to take it with him. He checks the phone and sees six missed calls and three voice mail messages. Three calls are from Craig, one from Laura, one unknown number and one from Mark. He listens to the voice mails; the first is from Craig, thanking him for the good news on Peter's confession. The second is from Mark, asking him to call him back. The third is another message from Craig, also asking him to call him back.

He calls Mark first. When he answers, he asks if everything is OK. Mark tells him, 'Thanks for calling back, I just wanted to let you know my train and others have been cancelled until further notice. The police are dealing with an incident on the line, between Haughley junction and Stowmarket.

There's also a problem with the overhead electric power supply between Ipswich and Manningtree. Greater Anglia is trying to source some replacement buses, to take us

Suffolk's Last Cold War Victim

to Colchester station for our onward journey. I'll give you a call when I get to my office.'

Ashley thanks him for the update and said, 'If you want to come back to the village give me a call.' The next call is to Laura, who told him she only wanted to know if he needed anything from the shops on her way round.

He tries ringing Craig, but all he keeps getting is an engaged tone. When he finally gets through, he asks, 'Hi Craig, how's it going your end?'

'It's all very intense here at the moment. Information is coming in thick and fast, I'm struggling to keep up with it all. I listened to your message; the confession would've made things a lot easier, but it's not required now.' Ashley interrupts and asks what he meant, "not required"?

Craig explains, 'This is still to be confirmed, but we believe at 11:45 am this morning, Peter walked into the path of an express train, just north of Stowmarket station.

His van's been found on the B1113 Stowmarket road, close to the railway line. We've sent the local bobby round to inform his father his son may be the deceased man.' Ashley shouts, 'Oh my god…What a frightful mess this is turning out to be for the Colonel's family.'

Craig continues, 'I agree, but we have to keep moving on until it's been confirmed. I've been asked by Forensics, if you'll show them the exact location of the nuclear shelter. If so will it OK for them to pick you up?'

Suffolk's Last Cold War Victim

He replies, 'That's fine, as long as I can take Laura with me. I don't want her to be left alone at the moment.' Craig agrees, 'I'll authorise that for you. They should be with you in about an hour's time. I'll make sure it's an unmarked car. When news of Brian's death is released, I don't want any curtain twitchers see you getting into a police car and link you with his death.

Would it be OK for me to stay at yours for another night? Tomorrow I'll be coordinating the surveillance team on the plan to apprehend the gang at either the Farmhouse or Cambridge airport.' Ashley tells him he is more than welcome to stay another night.

The doorbell rings Ashley goes to open the door hoping its Laura. Suddenly he remembers 11:45 am, the time Craig said Peter allegedly committed suicide. This is the exact time he dropped Mark off at the station and when he felt something bad had happened.

'Hello Laura so glad to see you, so much has happened since this morning. Firstly, the police are on the way to pick me up. I'm going to take them to the nuclear shelter. They've agreed I can take you along, but only if you want to.

Secondly, this morning I met Colonel Hungerford and told him the police had information of Peter's involvement in Brian's disappearance. When he confronted him this news, Peter told him he was going to hand himself in to the police. Instead of going to a police station, he drove to a high-speed rail line and walked in front of an express train.'

Suffolk's Last Cold War Victim

He sees Laura's lips begin to quiver, she does not know what to say or do. Ashley does, he holds her tight as she burst into tears. He reassures her and says, 'I think we should say a prayer for everyone who's been affected by today's events.'

'Thank you, Ashley, that's exactly what we should do, and I want to include Peter in our prayers as well. And yes, I'll go with you, I'd need to see Godpop's tomb.'

There was just enough time to phone Mark to give him an update and call Colonel Hungerford.

The Colonel tells him, 'I've just had the police round. They told me Peter's van's been found near a rail line, close to where a person was killed by a train. I know it's him, that's why he didn't want me to go with him.

As soon as the body's been formally identified, my wife and I are going to stay with our daughter Sophie in Buxton. We'd planned to move there until Peter came back to live with us again. We can't live around here anymore; I'll get an estate agent round to put the house on the market tomorrow. I'll give you a call later when I've some more information.' He thanks the Colonel for letting him know and said his thoughts are with his family at such a sad time for them.

The police car arrives to pick them up a few minutes later. It did not take very long to arrive at the place Brian showed him last week. The officer thanks him for his assistance in locating the shelter, but now the site has to be sealed off to allow forensics to do their job.

Suffolk's Last Cold War Victim

He said he will take them back home. As the weather is warm and sunny, Ashley asks the officer if they can be dropped off in Kelway. The officer obliges and twenty minutes later they are walking towards their favourite meadow. Ashley takes off his jacket and lays it on the grass for Laura to sit on.

He tells her he wants to bring her here, for the peace and quiet it affords them. She said, 'I agree, there's so many things happening at the moment.' He continues, 'We need to talk so we can start making plans for our future, as friends or something more, if that's what you want too. Never in a million years did I think I'd be able to move on so soon after Susan's death. But I believe she's somehow pushing me into having someone I can be physically close to, does that make any sense to you?'

She replies 'That makes perfect sense to me. I too am getting the same vibes from Philip.'

Ashley takes her hand, 'Two weeks ago, I was a frightened, lonely man, who only had two friends I could count on. Then I heard you playing the church organ and when you spoke to me, my dark clouds began to clear. Why was that? I didn't know anything about you. Were you married, in a relationship, did you have children? All I knew was, I wanted to learn more about you.

What happens in the future, I can't be sure, but one thing I know for sure, we're way past first base as friends. Susan was the only woman I've been with, so I may need some pointers along the way.' Laura squeezes his hand and said, 'Me too' before giving him a peck on the lips.

Suffolk's Last Cold War Victim

Their peace is broken when he receives a text message from Craig saying he will be home in an hour's time. This gives them just enough time to walk home. On the way Mark texted to say he has finally arrived back in his office, and he will call him later this evening for a catch up.

They arrive home five minutes before Craig got there. When he enters the house he asks, 'Can I treat you both to dinner at the pub or would you prefer a takeaway? I've got so much to tell you.'

Laura and Ashley agree it's probably better to have a takeaway, as they did not want anyone overhearing them in the pub. As they wait for their meal to arrive, Ashley walks to the Co-op to buy some bottles of beer.

Following their chicken curry meal, Craig is enjoying a glass of Ghost Ship when his phone rings; it's a colleague working on Brian's case. Realising the sensitivity, he tells them he will take it in his bedroom.

When he returns, he tells them, 'Brian's body's been found exactly as he told us. The scenes of crime team have been given permission to remove his body for a postmortem. The preliminary examination gave asphyxiation as the cause of death. They also found a card in the shelter addressed to Laura Archibald; they hope to release it to you tomorrow.

Whilst we're on the subject of Brian, Peter Hungerford's body has been positively identified. His mobile phone records showed he was in the vicinity on the day Brian went missing. Blood samples and fingerprints are being examined and CCTV shows him purchasing the torch, found in

Suffolk's Last Cold War Victim

the shelter. With Brian's testament and Peter's confession to his father, this case should be wrapped up fairly quickly.

My investigation's also going well. We've discovered a private jet has been charted from Cambridge airport to Majorca on Wednesday afternoon. The farmhouse is under 24/7 armed surveillance. We'll wait until they're on the open tarmac and about to board the jet, before we go in to arrest them.

I've also been in touch with the fraud squad regarding Rogers. They've spoken to Colson, who said he'll help us with our investigation, without asking for any concessions from us. He can't abide the man and his tactics.

Our team, as well as Mark's men, will be in the Heathlands pub tomorrow evening and hopefully, they'll get some incriminating evidence on him.'

As promised, Mark calls to see how things are going. Ashley said, 'Everything seems to be happening all at once. The only thing I know for certain, Brian's become Suffolk's last Cold War victim. I think it's best to hear the rest from Craig. I'll give you a call tomorrow mate.' He passes his phone to Craig.

Ashley asks Laura if she wants to go into the garden for a bit of fresh air. He did not want her hearing any unpleasant details about her Godpop's death.

She agrees, they take their glasses outside and sit at the garden table. They watch the sun slowly disappearing to the west and listen to the birds singing for the last time in April.

Suffolk's Last Cold War Victim

Twenty minutes later, Craig joins them outside. Handing back the phone he comments, 'This is so beautiful and quiet, I'd love to live somewhere like this. Mark's now fully up to date with today's events. He wants to know if he can use your comment "Suffolk's last Cold War victim" as the headline for a story he wants to run this Sunday. Can you let him know tomorrow?'

Ashley asks how Brian's death is going to be reported in the press. Craig tells him, 'Police will be holding a press conference at Martlesham HQ tomorrow morning. The statement will say, 'A man suspected of causing the death of another man by locking him in a derelict underground shelter, has been killed after walking into the path of a train on Monday 30th April. Both men lived in the same village and are known to each other. The motives for both deaths are still being investigated.' There will be no mention of the birthday card or the lottery ticket inside it.

The rest of the evening is spent relaxing with a few drinks and talking about the nuances of the Suffolk dialect. Ashley tells them, 'I reckon it's going to take a lot longer for me to be Suffolkated now I'm going to lose Brian.' Quick as a flash Laura says, 'Thas awl roight, Oy'll larn yer Suffolk.' It turns out Laura is as fluent in the dialect as her teacher, one Brian Damant. She agrees to stay the night with him again, but this time in the spare bedroom.

Craig is up and out very early the next morning, as he wants to gather more intelligence on the gang. Over breakfast, Ashley asks Laura what her plans are for the day.

Suffolk's Last Cold War Victim

She tells him she is going to see her Headmaster to explain the reason for her absence.

They agree to meet up in the church after lunch, as she wants to say a prayer for Brian. He walks to the shops to stock up on his groceries and see if anyone knows about Brian and Peter's deaths. It's not long before he sees and hears groups of people talking about both of them.

He really wants to talk to the Hungerford's, to see how they are coping. On the way back he walks to their house, but it has been cordoned off with forensic police officers going in and out. He decides to give the Colonel a call later on this evening.

He has only been home for a few minutes when he receives a call from Mark. 'Hi Ashley, hope you and Laura are OK? I've just listened to the press conference on Brian and Peter's deaths; I don't think there'll be much interest from the national press, as they don't know about the lottery ticket motive.

We of course, won't disclose it either. However, we want to use the story of their deaths, together with the number of nuclear shelters still dotted around Suffolk. That's why I'd like to use your comments for our headline on Sunday, if that's OK with you?' Ashley tells him he is welcome to use it and looks forward to reading the story. They agree to talk again tomorrow, following 'Rogers' meeting this evening.

He makes himself a sandwich, before heading out to meet Laura at the church. He is surprised to see several

Suffolk's Last Cold War Victim

villagers in and outside the church, talking about the terrible events.

Inside he sees Laura talking with a large group of people, he recognises many of them. They are really upset on hearing the news and begin speculating on the cause of their deaths.

After saying a prayer for the deceased, many said they would meet up again this evening and have a drink to Brian in the pub.

When he gets her on his own he tells her, 'Craig called to say he's coming to collect his things at 18:00 pm and wants me to ensure you'll be there as he has something for you.'

There was a period of anxious trepidation as the clock passes 18:30 pm. They are both wondering why he's late, what does he have for her, could it be bad news on the gang's capture? They need not have worried, when he arrives he explains, 'Sorry I'm late. Traffic's manic out there. I can't stop long, I've got to be in Cambridge by 21:00 pm, but I personally wanted to give this to you.' He opens his briefcase and pulls out an envelope addressed to Laura Archibald and a set of keys. 'The keys are to Brian's house. Forensics will be going in tomorrow, after they've finished you can go in.'

He hands them to her and said, 'I read the card as part of the investigation and I've got to say, it really made me sad and happy at the same time. When we finally catch the bad boys, I hope to see you both and have a well-earned drink.' With that he departs.

Suffolk's Last Cold War Victim

Laura keeps fondling the envelope, picking it up, putting it down. Ashley asks if she would like him to read it to her. She says, 'Yes please.'

As he opens the envelope a euro lottery ticket fell out. He looked at the date, Tuesday 27th March, and on the back was Laura's name and address. The card read, 'Happy Birthday to my wonderful Goddaughter', with a big bunch of pink roses on it.

Inside Brian had written:

"This is addressed to my wonderful Goddaughter Laura Archibald. I bet you thought I'd forgotten your birthday for the first time in your life? Well, I haven't. It's just this postman's was locked in a small shelter by Peter Hungerford on Wednesday 28th March 2018. I don't know if I'll be rescued in time to save my life. If you read this card, you'll know it's too late for me.

This'll come as a big shock when I tell you I'm your biological father. Your mum and dad tried for a long time to conceive but couldn't. They asked me to be a sperm donor. When you were born, I was the proudest man in the world and I still am.

The lottery ticket is worth one million pounds. When you speak to Camelot, tell them I bought the ticket as a gift for your birthday, but it was late being delivered.

You are also the sole beneficiary of my will. You'll find it in a small safe behind your picture, in my living room. The

Suffolk's Last Cold War Victim

code is 24041973. Enjoy your life; I love you so much, from your Godpop."

When he finished reading the card, Laura grabs hold of Ashley, hugging him tight and crying uncontrollably for the next five minutes. When Ashley asks what she is thinking, she replies, 'I never knew any of this before I read your notes. Now I know everything you wrote and said on Sunday must be true. You weren't even in the village when he wrote the card. This means the messages from Philip, Susan and Jason must be true as well. I need a drink. Let's go and toast my dad in the pub.'

The pub is packed full of people from in and around the village. There's only one person they are talking about, and it's certainly not Peter Hungerford.

As expected, Colonel Hungerford is nowhere to be seen. Ashley tries to phone him, but it goes straight to voice mail. He leaves a message saying his thoughts are with him and his family and asks the Colonel to give him a call when he's ready.

The first to greet Ashley and Laura is Trevor Sharp; he said how sorry he is for the death of her Godfather. The talk then touched on to the shelter where he was found. Sharpie said he knew the location, as he used to visit it regularly when he was in the army.

Ashley tells him, 'A journalist friend of mine is going to write a story about these nuclear shelters. If you provide him with some information on their locations and use, he'll

Suffolk's Last Cold War Victim

pay you a lot of money.' Sharpie said, 'If my name's not revealed and the price is right, I'd be glad to help.'

Ashley walks a few steps away and phones Mark to see if he is interested in talking to Sharpie. He is very interested and takes his phone number and promised to give him a call. Sharpie's phone is ringing before Ashley gets back to join him. By the look on his face, he is more than happy with Mark's offer.

As people began to drift away Laura asks if she can stay with him again tonight. She is still very upset and he has been so supportive. He tells her she can stay with him for as long as she wants.

Suffolk's Last Cold War Victim

Chapter 22

Peace at last

Wednesday 2nd May is a beautiful, sunny and warm day. Yesterday was an eventful day for Laura. For Ashley, this is the day he has been waiting a long time for.

Over breakfast they talk about things they have to do. Laura said she has to contact Camelot to claim her prize and fetch some more clothes. After that, all she wants is sit and talk with him.

He said he is feeling very nervous, thinking of all the things that could go wrong with the police operation this afternoon. Laura, sensing his anxiety said, 'Right mister, I'm going to make the call to Camelot tomorrow. In the meantime, I'm going home to get some clean clothes and pick up some groceries for a picnic. While I'm doing that, you go and get the boat ready. We're going on a trip, where there's no people and no mobile phones until four o'clock, when it should be all over. If it's good news we'll celebrate. If not, well let's wait and see.'

An hour later with the picnic stowed on board, they set off rowing up stream. Ashley reasoned it will be easier and quicker going with the flow on the way back. It was so peaceful, with only each other for company. He has been rowing gently for just under an hour, when they spot a perfect place for a picnic.

Suffolk's Last Cold War Victim

The water is just deep enough for the boat to moor alongside a large grassy bank. A large willow tree provides perfect shading from the sun. They lay a large blanket out on the grass and make themselves comfortable.

Laura notices he keeps looking at his watch every few minutes. She makes him take it off and hand it over until 16:00 pm, when the operation should be finished. Only then does he start to relax and talk about his dreams for the future. She is grateful and relieved to find most of them involve her.

When it is her turn, Ashley asks what she intends to do with lottery money. She said, 'When you buy a ticket, you've a good idea where it's going to be spent, but in this instance I honestly haven't a clue.'

'But if you'd bought the winning ticket yourself, what would you've spent the money on?' he asks.

'My ambitions would've been to pay off my mortgage, go travelling and be a volunteer teacher in some remote African village.'

He said, 'You can still do all those things, plus I can go with you and write a book about it.' She agrees and said she would like that. After finishing the picnic, they go for a walk across a meadow heading towards a church spire.

She wants to look inside the church, whilst he is hoping to find a pub, as he's desperate for a strong drink to settle his nerves. But more importantly a toilet, he's one fart away from following through.

Suffolk's Last Cold War Victim

Luckily, both their wishes are answered and an hour later they begin the return journey to Belford, most of which is in silence. He calculated the time by the position of the sun and knows it's close to 16:00 pm.

As they pull alongside the pontoon, Laura hands back his watch; he is only ten minutes off the correct time. Entering the house, he turns on his mobile. Disappointingly there are no missed calls or text messages from Craig.

Just as he begins to feel deflated, the phone rings. When he sees its Craig calling him he nearly drops it as his hands begin to shake. Laura gets him to sit down and take some deep breaths. He said, 'Hello Craig. Is it good or bad news?'

'Mate, it couldn't have gone any better. We've got them all, including the money. They'll be processed before being sent to high security prisons tonight. Ashley, are you all right mate? Talk to me.' This time it was Laura who hugged him whilst he cries and is unable to talk. She takes the phone off him and tells Craig 'He's fine, he'll call you back shortly.

Within two minutes of this call, his phone rings again; it's Mark who has just been told the news as well. Ashley has calmed down just enough to be able to talk to his friend.

'Mark, we've done it, we've got them. I was worried all last night and today that something was going to go wrong. But now all I want to do is kiss somebody.'

And that's exactly what he did. He held Laura and asked if it was OK for him to kiss her. She said, 'Yes please.' So

Suffolk's Last Cold War Victim

he did while Mark was still speaking. 'Ashley, are you still there? Hello Ashley...never mind. I'll call you back later.'

As they break off from kissing, Ashley asks, 'What's happening to us? I don't feel guilty for doing that, do you?' She did not say anything; she just grabs hold and kisses him again.

Feeling composed, he rings Craig to congratulate him and his team on the great work they done leading up to today's arrests.

Thirty minutes later, he calls Mark back to ask if his reporters managed to film the police operations. An immensely proud Mark answers, 'We recorded the whole operation which went like clockwork. The look of shock on their faces was priceless. Needless to say it'll be the headline story in tomorrow's 'Everyday News'. Trevor Sharp is also playing a blinder. He's certainly an expert on nuclear shelters and we're confident we'll do Brian proud in our Sunday edition.

Also last night, we got some good film footage of Rogers with the hired thug; he's certainly one son of a bitch. All in all, it's been one hell of week for you, Laura and the village. When the date of Brian's funeral has been agreed, please let me know as Craig and I would like to attend and pay our respects.'

Ashley said, 'Thanks for all your support I couldn't have wished for a better friend through all the dark times of late. You and Craig are invited to stay with me, when the funeral date has been confirmed.

Suffolk's Last Cold War Victim

When they woke on Thursday morning, their mood feels different from the last few days. They are relaxed and easy in each other's company now everything's out in the open.

The only thing outstanding today is for her to contact Camelot to claim her prize. When she makes the call she asks him to sit with her. Needless to say, that's exactly what he did.

The procedure is quite easy; they took her details and said they will call her back shortly. When they did, they said they will send a representative round to verify the ticket, give her some financial advice and confirm her bank details. Laura said she is available any day next week. As Monday is a bank holiday, they agree on Tuesday 8th May at 10:00 am.

On Friday morning Laura receives a phone call from the police, informing her forensics have finished their investigations and she can now enter Brian's house. Ashley said, 'I'll come with you whenever you're ready. She said, 'I'd like to go round this afternoon and have a good clear up.'

Entering the house, she starts to cry when she sees the state the police, or Hungerford have left it in. Ashley points to a picture of her on the living room wall. Behind the picture is a safe, just as Brian told them. He asks, 'Can you remember the code?'

She said, 'Of course I can, it's 24041973.' He asks, 'How did you remember that?' 'It's easy, that's my birthday.'

Inside the safe they find a copy of his last will and testament, the house deeds, two thousand pounds in cash,

Suffolk's Last Cold War Victim

Maggie's wedding ring, plus other bits of her jewellery, a cassette tape and a large envelope addressed to Laura.

Inside the envelope she finds a letter and a prepaid funeral plan. He has left instructions on the order of service, songs and an inscription he wants to go on their joint head stone.

They spend the rest of the day and most of the evening clearing and tidying every room. She leaves one room till last. It's the bedroom she used when she stayed with her Godparents. When she enters the room, it felt like she has gone back forty years to her childhood. All the toys she played with are still there, the sight of them brought more tears.

On Saturday morning Craig phones, 'I've called to let you know, Vasil Petrov and Stoyan Ivanor have been charged with the murders of Susan and Jason. The other three have been charged with conspiracy to murder. The trials are scheduled to take place in October.

I've also got some news on the drink spiking case. The local police have made three arrests for numerous drug offences. Undercover policemen followed a number of suspects during the evening and three youths were caught red handed spiking other youth's drinks, including Melvin's. Melvin however, was unaware of the arrests and appears to have had an enjoyable evening.

Personally I've received some good news, I'm being commended for my part in the gang's arrest and my boss has put me up for promotion to Superintendent. Ashley says,

Suffolk's Last Cold War Victim

'Thanks for the update and congratulation on your good news, you deserve it.'

Ashley and Laura enjoyed a peaceful and restful weekend. Saturday evening was spent in the pub with the usual crowd. On Sunday they attend the church service, with Laura playing the organ. A lot more villagers than usual are in attendance.

After they got home from the church service, they read The World of News story of Suffolk's last Cold War victim. The story revealed the deaths of Brian and Peter Hungerford and the nuclear shelters, still posing a danger after all these years.

On Tuesday, while waiting for the Camelot representative to arrive, Laura made appointments with Brian's chosen Funeral Director and Solicitor. Both are booked for tomorrow morning.

The meeting with the Rep was quite straightforward. There were a few questions on how she obtained the ticket, did she want to keep anonymity, her bank details and did she want any financial advice. The rep tells her the money will be in her bank account before the end of the week.

The meetings on Wednesday are just formalities, as Brian has crossed all the T's and dotted the I's. Whilst sitting in James Arnott, the Funeral Directors waiting room, Laura receives a call from the Coroner's office. They have agreed to release his body for burial. Their timing was perfect, as it saved her making another appointment.

Suffolk's Last Cold War Victim

Mr Arnott welcomes her, 'Good morning Laura, please take a seat. I'm so sorry for your sad loss of your Godfather. As you're aware Brian made his funeral arrangements with me a few weeks ago. He was anxious to get it done quickly due to his terminal Prostate cancer diagnosis. His Oncologist told him he only had another six months to live, and then this happened.

A shocked Laura asks, 'Prostate cancer, that's the first I've heard of it. So he knew he only had six months to live.' Mr Arnott answers, 'I'm the only person he told, he didn't want anyone feeling sorry for him. Anyway, here is his comprehensive order of service. All we need now is a date.'

Laura says, 'As it happens, while I was in the waiting room, I got a call from the Coroner's office to say they've released his body for burial

Opening his diary he said, 'Their timing's perfect, these are some of the dates available. Have a look at them, while I make a quick call to arrange for someone to go and collect him' Laura looks at the dates, when he returns she replies, 'I'd like to book Friday 18th May if I may.' Mr Arnott writes the date in his diary before confirming, 'Ok that's all booked. If you've any further questions please give me a call. Thanks for coming in.

At the meeting with Elena Butunoiu, his Solicitor, she read out Brian's last will and testament, confirming Laura as the sole benefactor. When the Grant of Probate has been issued she will inherit the house including all fittings and furnishings, his bank accounts and his life insurance policies.

Suffolk's Last Cold War Victim

Friday 18th May is beautiful sunny day, perfect weather for Brian's funeral taking place today. The church is packed full of mourners from the surrounding villages, who he served for many years as their postman. Both Mark and Craig are here to pay their respects and looking forward to toasting him at the wake afterwards.

The only variation to the order of service Brian planned is a medley of his favourite songs, played by Laura on the church's organ. Ashley tells his friends, 'That's a lovely touch from his daughter.'

At the wake in the Belford Arms, Laura welcomes everybody and says, 'Thank you all for the lovely flowers and messages today. I'm unable to put into words the things I want to say about my Godpop, but I know a man who can. She presses play on a cassette recorder.

The tape crackles before Brian's voice announces,

'Oy'd jest loike ter thank yoo awl fer cumm'n...boy neow yoo'll realoise...Oy'm dead'n gorn...Oy ent goo'na rattle on fer too long.

Oy've 'ad a good loife...but neow Oy'm with moy Maggie agin...Oy'm soo happy. Oy want yoo awl ter git yerself a point...Moycrow has agreed ter pay '

There is a small pause before he continues.

'Sumbody gitt 'em up orf the flawer!...Oy've put some money behind the baar. Jest afore Oy goo...if anyone aasks where Oy've gorn...wotta yoo awl goo'na say?!'

Suffolk's Last Cold War Victim

Everyone in the pub points to Adrian Harris, [standing at the bar] and calls out in unison, "FOK knows!"

Brian finishes with, 'Luv yoo awl...cheerio tergither.'

There's not a dry eye in the pub after his farewell speech.

Ashley, half expects Brian to turn up in some form to say, 'Gotcha,' but he never did.

Suffolk's Last Cold War Victim

Chapter 23

Password to paradise

On 29th March 2019, the anniversary of Brian's death, Laura and Ashley are in the churchyard, sitting on a bench dedicated to his memory. They are reminiscing on all the things that have happened to them and the village over the past year.

Ashley remembers how he was made to feel welcome from the day he arrived. He has made some great friends, no more so than the woman sitting next to him.

The village youth club has been built and equipped with money donated by an anonymous benefactor. The youth club is being run by a husband-and-wife team, Colin and Nicola Scott. In June she resigned as a Conservative councillor and Chairperson on the Planning Committee. She fell on her sword because of a poor decision she made, when recommending acceptance for a planning application made by a crooked businessman. Her husband has been really supportive of her ever since.

Following a long investigation into his Property Development business, Steve Rogers was found guilty on a number of fraud and bribery cases. He received a 12 year prison sentence. Barry Colson provided the prosecution with information on his hidden accounts .The accounts he used to fund the bribe money.

Suffolk's Last Cold War Victim

A number of civil servants and local councillors were also implicated for accepting bribes from Rogers. Many received prison sentences or large fines. All these men and women lost their jobs as a consequence.

The hired thug, who was filmed taking a bribe in Ipswich, received a four-year prison sentence. He had been used by Rogers on a number of other cases.

Colonel Hungerford sold his house and moved to be near his daughter in Buxton. He never returned any of Ashley's calls. Trevor Sharp said Colonel Hungerford blames himself for his son's actions. Sharpie is worried about his mental health. Every time he phones him he keeps repeating, 'If only I hadn't taken him to the shelters when he was a boy, things might have turned out differently.'

Laura allows Glenn and Kat to live rent free in Brian's house, whilst they continue saving for a deposit. This will take longer than they planned, as Glenn is currently training to be a Train Driver. This means his wages will be a lot lower until he qualifies.

They are unaware in three years time Laura is going to give them the house. This will be a big a thank you present, for all the help Glenn gave Laura after the death Philip. Kat and Glenn asked Laura if she will be a Godmother to their first born. She agreed with one proviso, her old room must be used as a nursery.

Craig Ferguson received a commendation for his work in recapturing the gang. He was also promoted to Superintendent and is now based at Martlesham Heath

Suffolk's Last Cold War Victim

Constabulary Headquarters. He relocated his wife and two teenage daughters to a village less than two miles from Belford. His family loves the country lifestyle, and the girls are doing well at their new school.

He has used Ashley's 'gift' on two occasions. Once when investigating a particularly gruesome murder of a dog walker in Rendlesham Forest. The other involved the apparent suicide of an elderly woman, who died from an overdose of prescribed tablets in her home. In both cases he helped provide a vital snippet of information from the victims', something the police had overlooked in their initial investigations.

Melvin Gale dodged having his drink spiked in the Woodbridge nightclub and has been doing very well at university.

The three youths involved in spiking drinks, all admitted the charges against them and received lengthy community service sentences.

Bill –Micro- Gates' health problems did not get any worse, but his doctor still advised him to cut down on his workload. So, he employed Perry Lakeman to run the pub at the weekends. Perry loves being back behind the bar and so do the customers. Bill uses his time off to go freshwater fishing around the county.

Ashley was tempted to become a professional clairvoyant using his 'gift'. Although he believes he would do well, the timing is not right for him and Laura at the moment.

Suffolk's Last Cold War Victim

The trial of the infamous five produced guilty verdicts on all counts of murder and conspiracy to murder. Vasil Petrov and Stoyan Ivanor were both given an additional ten years, on top of their original sentences. Trevor Bannister, Penka Georgieva and Maria Georgieva received an extra five years.

Both Mark Haines and Craig Ferguson had another honour to perform in February. Mark gave the bride away and Craig was best man at Ashley and Laura's wedding.

Laura sold her house and moved in with Ashley after their wedding. They have travelled to some of the poorest countries in Africa, to help educate young children in remote villages, using the money from the sale of her house and Ashley's savings.

Laura has not used any of the lottery money for herself, knowing the circumstances behind it. She did however give half of it to Brian and Maggie's nieces and nephews on both sides of their families. The remaining sum is in a joint account, only to be used in an emergency.

Their next expedition will see them travel to a remote village in Ethiopia, where they will be working with a well-known children's charity to build a school in a small village. She will teach English to the children, and he will help with the building work and write an account of the operations for his friend Mark's Sunday newspaper.

Mark Haines was named 'Editors' Editor of the Year' for the stories of the capture of the criminal gang, and highlighting the dangers of derelict nuclear shelters in Suffolk.

Suffolk's Last Cold War Victim

Ashley finished his book based on the stories of the village and its inhabitants. However he decided not to publish it, he thought people would think it's too farfetched.

After they finished reminiscing, Laura looks at her husband, he has a quizzical look on his face. She asks, 'Darling what's bothering you?'

He says, 'It's nothing big, as we were reminiscing about the past something reminded me of an unanswered question I had at Brian's wake.' She asks, 'Tell me what it is and perhaps I can help solve it for you.'

He said, 'Ok here goes. It's to do with the tape you played to us. With Micros poor health how did Brian know he was going to go before him? I told you it isn't a big thing.' She grabs his hand and squeezes it gently and says, 'I said I could help, Brian had terminal Prostate cancer, he knew he only had six months to live. When he was with James Arnott, sorting out his funeral plans. He told about his prognosis, he was the only person that knew. I wish I'd told you this earlier' He said, 'I wish I'd asked you earlier. It makes perfect sense to me now. Thank you.'

Laura stands and asks, 'I'm just going in to have a practice on the organ. Do you want to come in?' He said, 'As it's such a lovely day, I'd like sit and listen to you playing from here.'

He closes his eyes as he listens to her playing. Something made him open his eyes. He is shocked to see his old friend Brian sitting on the seat next to him.

Suffolk's Last Cold War Victim

'Brian, what on earth are you doing here, I thought you passed over last year.'

Brian replies, 'Oy've bin troy'n to…but Oy caarn't git through…Oy reck'n Oy needa paaswud ter git theyer.'

Ashley has no problem understanding what he just said, as his wife has "wholly Suffolkated" him during the past year.

He's really missed listening to his stories, even the wind-ups, but senses his friend is suffering deeply, not being able to finally be reunited with his beloved Maggie.

It takes a few minutes before Ashley exclaims, 'Brian that's it, you said you needed a password. I think I know what that password is.

You once told me, if I ever said the name of that place north of Diss, I'd never see you again. Well, my old friend, I hope this works and in the nicest possible way, I hope I never see you again.'

He closes his eyes and says, 'That word is NORWICH.' When he opens his eyes again, Brian has gone.

And to his great relief, he never saw him again.